DECK THE MANE

A LION'S PRIDE #14

EVE LANGLAIS

Deck the Mane © 2022 Eve Langlais

Cover Art by Yocla Designs © 2022

Produced in Canada

Published by Eve Langlais

http://www.EveLanglais.com

E-ISBN: 978 1 77 384 335 3
Print ISBN: 978 1 77 384 336 0

All Rights Reserved

This book is a work of fiction and the characters, events and dialogue found within the story are of the author's imagination and are not to be construed as real. Any resemblance to actual events or persons, either living or deceased, is completely coincidental.

No part of this book may be reproduced or shared in any form or by any means, electronic or mechanical, including but not limited to digital copying, file sharing, audio recording, email and printing without permission in writing from the author.

CHAPTER ONE

ON THE FIRST DAY OF CHRISTMAS, MY TRUE LOVE GAVE TO ME - A MIRROR SO WE COULD ADMIRE OUR LUSCIOUS MANE.

Felix took a moment to check his hair. Perfect. As usual. Summoned to his mother's presence, he'd dressed casually in tweed trousers, a buttoned shirt, and loafers with no socks. He might go for a stroll in town later and give the people a thrill that their prince walked among them. Maybe stop for a fresh coffee and a catnip-sprinkled donut.

Mother had other plans.

"Pack a bag. You're going on a trip. You're to leave within the hour. The jet is waiting."

"Leave for where?" Felix asked his mother.

The matriarch of his family, and current head of the Pride in Spain, she was splendid despite having celebrated her sixtieth birthday. Her natural hair was more gray than gold, but her face remained mostly smooth, and not because of surgery. Lion genetics played a part, but she also religiously moisturized, as did he.

"You are going to America. You'll be spending Christmas with your cousin Arik." Mother slipped into impeccable English. They all spoke without a hint of an accent. Part of their education.

Before a confused Felix could ask why, his sister, a mini-me version of his mother, swept in. "Did you tell him?"

"How does she know before me?" He stabbed a finger in his sibling's direction, the rivalry between them alive and well.

"Don't whine. It's not attractive," Mother chided.

"I will whine if I want, given my own flesh and blood is ridding themselves of me this holiday season." Felix clutched his chest. "So unloved."

"Don't be a drama lion. It wasn't on purpose. It just so happens I've got plans, and as queen-in-waiting, your sister has been invited to spend Christmas with the Italian Pride as part of our treaty negotiations. You should thank me for ensuring you won't be alone."

"It's twelve days until Christmas. What am I supposed to do?"

"Reconnect with your American cousins. Eat some of their cuisine."

"I'd hardly call their chain of steakhouses cuisine." His lip curled.

"I hear it's quite good." Mother kept countering his arguments. "While there, you can finish up negotiations on our upcoming merger with Arik. Oh, you should try and visit Honey Pine Farm."

"Why would I do that?"

"Because they have some very unique honey, and if you could score me a jar of Honey-Wrinkle-No, you'd be my favorite son."

"I'm you're only son."

"For now." A dumb threat since mother had no intention of having more kids.

"Do you know how cold it is in America this time of year?" Felix exclaimed. "Think of the havoc it will wreak on my mane." He gave his golden locks a little shake.

His sister, standing alongside his mother, sporting the same disapproving scowl, snorted. "Vain idiot."

"You really shouldn't frown like that, sister dear. Wrinkles are everyone's enemy. If you'd like, I can recommend a cream. It might not be too late for you."

"I will skin you," his sister hissed.

"Now, children." Mother stepped in. "We don't have time for arguing. I have spoken."

And that was that.

Felix barely had time to pack all his essentials before being whisked to the airport. He spent the second day of Christmas at a high altitude, eating chocolate-covered strawberries and drowning his sorrows in wine. Not enough for a hangover. After all, he wanted to look his best.

A prearranged vehicle waited when he arrived,

driven by an old acquaintance. Leo was a massive man who'd gotten bigger since they'd last seen each other. Married life agreed with him obviously. He filled Felix in on the most recent news as he drove to his cousin's base of operations, a condominium complex that housed a good chunk of his pride.

Given America's massive size and population, more than a few lion groups existed, each with their own king, but Cousin Arik's was the most powerful. And rich. The man made a fortune in hair products, among other things.

"Afraid I'll have to drop you and run. I'm having dinner with my mate, no kids, and she threatened to neuter me if I'm late." With those words, Leo deposited Felix at the front of the condo building, luggage piled on the sidewalk. Only six bags since he'd barely had time to pack. He'd have to do some shopping. With Mother's credit card, of course.

Felix gave his hair a finger comb before entering and announcing, "Rejoice, my American cousins, for I am here to make your holiday season glorious and bright." Felix stood majestically, waiting to be acknowledged by the sprawling lionesses on the many divans scattered throughout the common area in the lobby.

Only one set of eyes turned his way. Then the woman with the multicolored hair achieved through copious amounts of bleach—horrifying! —yawned and turned away.

Perhaps they'd not heard him, or they had something wrong with their vision? Must be. How else could they not see his greatness?

He struck a more flattering pose and tried again. "Ahem. It is I, Felix Charlemagne, visiting from far, far away Spain. Rejoice for we are about to spend Christmas together."

"Shhh. Can't you see Annabelle and Junior are napping!" A woman with extremely blonde hair—thankfully naturally occurring—wearing athletic gear, shushed him and pointed to a woman splayed on a couch with a baby sprawled across her chest.

"Too late," the no-longer-sleeping mother grumbled. Indeed, a second later the infant squalled. Loudly. The treble almost upset the perfect balance in Felix's hair. Good thing he'd double moisturized that morning.

"Do you know how long it took to settle him?" complained another woman, standing up and putting her hands on her hips. He recognized Joan, seeing as how she'd driven him from the airport the last time he'd flown in for a visit.

"He's colicky." Another woman confronted him with a scowl.

Finally, all eyes were upon Felix, and he tilted his chin, offering his best angle. "Fear not. I can put the child back to sleep."

"How? Going to bore him?" Asked with a roll of eyes. Such disrespect.

He'd show them. He snapped his fingers.

No one jumped. He almost sighed. How he missed home already, where his every whim was catered to before he even knew he had a whim.

"Hand over the child," he demanded.

"You planning to smother it? Because my husband has forbidden it." Annabelle grimaced at the yelling babe, who appeared to take after his lion father rather than his wolf mother, judging by his downy platinum hair.

"No need for drastic measures." He held out his hands, and the baby was placed in them.

He flipped the child to his shoulder and rubbed. The yodeling stilled immediately. A moment later, he handed back a sleeping cub.

The mother gaped at the baby, then him, and whispered, "How? It took me an hour of rocking, the skin off a nipple, and a prayer to the devil the last time."

He pulled out a small atomizer. "Spritz this on your clothes. It has a calming effect." He'd used it before disembarking the jet to ensure smooth entry via customs. A calm border agent didn't dig too deeply into his many hair products.

Annabelle snatched it. "Thank you."

"I'm going to need the name of the company so I can order a case. Might need some myself soon." A very pregnant female patted her rounded abdomen.

"Don't be foolish, cousin Luna. It is Luna, right?" He wasn't quite sure given they'd only met once during a previous family holiday and not gotten along well.

She'd shaved half his head. Of course, at the time they were both kids and he'd deserved it for telling her she had hair like that of a golden retriever.

"Aw, I'm touched you remember me, Weepy." His nickname that particular summer because he'd cried when he'd seen what she'd done to his head.

"The name is Felix, if you don't mind."

"I'll call you anything you like if you can get us more of that." She pointed at Annabelle and the spray bottle.

Someone tried to snatch it saying, "Let me have a sniff."

Annabelle bared her teeth and snarled, "Touch it and die."

Everyone chose to live.

It was one of the younger lounging felines who exclaimed, "Aren't you the guy in all those perfume commercials?"

About time they recognized him. He'd been aiming much of his media outreach at the younger demographics. "I am." He puffed his chest.

The slender female eyed him. "I thought you'd be taller."

He did his best to not glare. He'd not made it to thirty-five wrinkle free only to fail now. However, he did defend himself. "I am a respectable six foot two."

"Only?" That was the reply, followed by snickering.

No respect.

At all.

He'd forgotten the boldness of American females. Or, as this group liked to be called, the Biatches. Before he caused an international incident, he chose to excuse himself. "Ladies, while this has been an absolute pleasure, my cousin awaits." He made his exit, somewhat mollified when someone whispered, "He's got a nice ass."

"I guess you could always put a bag over his head." The quick retort deflated his ego.

He fought to not purse his lips as he stalked for the desk manned by a guard who appeared more interested in his phone than his job, although he did glance at Felix when he cleared his throat.

"Take me to Arik." Felix made the demand.

"Do you have an appointment?" the fellow dared to ask.

"As if I need one."

"You do."

Felix arched a brow. "Do you know who I am?"

"Someone without an appointment because I have nothing on my list for today." The guard smirked.

Felix took a breath through his nose to calm the irritation. No stress. No wrinkles. No flipping out. That was for the less evolved.

"I am Felix Charlemagne, and my cousin Arik personally invited me here to spend the holidays." Perhaps Felix would talk to his cousin about educating his Pride on how to treat guests of importance. The last time Arik came to Spain to see Felix's family, they'd had a literal red carpet waiting on the runway.

"Hold on a second, you're his cousin Icky?"

Felix stiffened. "It's actually pronounced Ixy." A stupid name used only by Arik that came about during the summers they'd spent together at camp. There was a time they'd been best friends. But then adulthood happened.

In the last twenty years, they'd grown apart and had only rarely crossed paths in the last decade. Last time Felix saw Arik the man had gotten married to a human. A hairdresser, too, which Felix did admire. How nice to have a wife understanding of the care and maintenance that needed to go into having an incredible mane.

Rumor had it Arik fathered two children, a boy and a girl. Felix had a pair of creatures he cared for, too. He called the red fish Big Red, and the blue one Big Blue. Easy to tell apart. He used an automated feeder when he had to leave town. He'd finally mastered the whole responsible-for-another-living-thing level. Big Red and Big Blue had just celebrated the one-year mark. A record.

"I thought you'd be taller," the guard stated, eyeing him up and down.

"I am the same height as Arik." The strain to not grimace would mean extra exfoliating later.

The dubious expression of the guard almost had him gnashing his perfect teeth. They'd better be impeccable given the number of times he saw a dentist a year.

"I'll ring the king and let him know you're coming up."

Such disrespect for a prince. Felix could have been king if he'd fought for it, but he'd watched his father work himself into an early grave, and before that happened, the constant scowling had left a permanent mark on his face. It didn't appeal to Felix, so when his sister showed an interest, he chose to not fight, which drove her insane, as she assumed he plotted to take the throne away. He had no such plan, but he did enjoy stoking her paranoia.

Let her have the title of queen. Felix didn't have time, not if he wanted to maintain his beautiful mane. It took much work each day to keep it healthy. He couldn't slow down now, not knowing his father had gone bald before thirty.

A lion with no mane. It was a nightmare. No wonder the man died young. That wouldn't be Felix.

Let his sister become the first unmarried Pride Queen for all of Spain. Although how long she'd remain single had people laying wagers. Everyone assumed she'd give in to the pressure to have a man by her side and provide heirs. Felix couldn't wait to see heads explode when they realized Francesca preferred to date women and had already confided, her lip curling in distaste, that his children would be the heirs since she had no intention of letting anything leech life from her body. Probably for the best given Francesca's lack of motherly instinct.

Still, her plan to use his children as heirs might backfire, given he'd not found anyone he wanted to bestow his precious seed upon. No one worthy of his great mane. No one that kept him intrigued past a dalliance or two.

Francesca hadn't given up hope on Felix, though, and neither had he. Surely somewhere a woman existed who could pass muster. The first important point being they had to have incredible hair. A tough one, but he'd met a few candidates with adequate locks. A little bit of help from him and he could have turned decent into epic.

However, why bother when most never passed his second requirement? Pass muster by his mother. Not an easy task. Only certain lineages would do.

The guard stuck him on an elevator and pressed the button for the penthouse. As they zoomed up, he mentally went through more of his list. Must have excellent taste in cheese. None of that processed orange crap. A designer clothes connoisseur. He did have an image to maintain, after all. She should either know how to cook fine meals or recognize quality and have them catered. A proper diet went a long way toward keeping those golden strands of his luscious.

The elevator stopped, and Felix smoothed his suit, raked his fingers through his perfectly layered locks, and rapped at the door, looking nonchalant for the door cam.

His cousin opened the door and smiled. "Ixy! It's been too long." Arik held open his arms and hugged him enthusiastically. It gave Felix a chance to sniff at his scalp. Hint of apple pie, very American. Some vanilla. Maybe a touch of lavender.

Arik drew back. "Like it? It's my new line of shampoo and conditioner. I call it The Lion Essentials."

"It's simple. I assume you're marketing it as your budget line."

Arik smirked. "Most expensive actually. The world is in a period of surplus, which means people will pay more to go back to the basics. Which you well know."

"We're about to release our most basic line of scents yet," Felix admitted. While Arik made his fortune mostly in hair products, the Charlemagnes were renowned perfumers who had also begun dabbling in body sprays and lotions.

"Have to say I'm excited about our upcoming joint project. Don't know how it took us so long to collaborate." The venture being a mix of the Charlemagnes' know-how when it came to scent and Arik's company with soap to create a revolutionary, and expensive, line of care products. "But it's too early to discuss business. It's been too long, cousin."

"It has." The honest truth? Seeing Arik brought back

memories of a more relaxed time in his life. "You appear to have done well." Unlike Leo with his well-fed paunch, Arik remained fit and his hair absolutely stupendous.

"Couldn't be happier. You should try the mated thing. It's been amazing."

The very thought made Felix's hair curl. Eep. He quickly changed the subject. "Where are the progeny? I'd like to meet—"

A Tasmanian devil came whipping out of nowhere, landing atop Felix's shoulders with a giggle, while a more solemn child approached with chubby arms upraised. As if Felix could refuse. He scooped the girl while the boy straddled his shoulders.

Arik beamed. "Meet Leda and Dale."

Beautiful children. Both with golden hair. The boy bore a blessed three crowns on his head. It led to a very drunken Felix later exclaiming, "He's got perfect hair. They both do. But that girl of yours...she will break many hearts." She'd clung to Felix and declared him pretty. Good taste for one so young.

"I'm a lucky man," Arik replied smugly.

"Indeed, you are."

"I have Kira to thank for that. Who would have thought a hairdressing mishap would lead to me becoming a husband and father." The woman in question had left the men to reminisce while she bathed and put the children to bed.

"Ah, the lovely Kira. You're so lucky." Felix sighed.

"For a human, she is rather perfect. Her hair, her manner, her laughter."

"Careful, Ixy," Arik warned.

"Never fear, cousin. I would never. But I have to say, seeing you with your brood is rather inspiring even as I fear it's impossible."

"You'll find the right person too, Ixy."

"Alas, dear cousin, that would take a Christmas miracle." Not likely with only ten days left until Christmas.

CHAPTER TWO

ON THE THIRD DAY OF BEARMAS, MY TRUE LOVE GAVE TO ME—NOTHING BECAUSE I AM NOT DATING THAT WOLF WHO THINKS IT'S FUNNY TO ASK IF I'M RELATED TO THE CHARMIN FELLOW.

"Merry Bearmas!" Edwina boomed as the many cars arrived, spilling lions all over the place for the annual tree hunt. It almost made her sneeze to have so many cats in close proximity. She never had that problem with the wolves, but at the same time, the wolves were cheap compared to the felines, always trying to haggle a lower price.

"And a Merry Christmas to you too," Luna declared, waddling over, her belly leading the way. So many of the Biatches had settled down in recent years. It roused a bit of jealousy in Edwina to see them with cubs. She'd always wanted a cuddly tyke she could hug and squish and call Little Eddy. Alas, she'd yet to meet her bear-fect match.

"You look ready to pop!" Edwina declared, eyed the protruding belly.

"Because it was due two days ago. It's refusing to come out." Luna glared at the hump. It jiggled in reply.

"I take it you don't know the sex?"

"Nope. The little bugger kept its legs shut tight so we couldn't see shit on the ultrasound. But enough about my stubborn fetus. I was sorry hear about your grandfather." Luna's lips turned down.

Edwina shrugged. "I guess it was only a matter of time. Although, given how long he held out, I'd begun to think he would live with me forever. But then he met that widow in Florida while on a visit with my parents and... well... you know how it goes."

"He finally turned into a snow bear," Luna commiserated.

"I don't suppose you could get them to invite my mom for a visit," Nexxie exclaimed, having overheard. She'd increased her piercings since Edwina last saw her and now had one going through her tongue.

"Can you handle being orphaned more than six months every year?" Edwina asked.

"I should be so lucky!" Nexxie enthused, crossing her fingers and looking to the sky in added prayer.

In some respects, Nexxie had it right. Edwina enjoyed not having an old and ornery bear grumbling she lived in a freezer. In her defense, no one should have their house heated to eighty-five.

No.

One.

Grandpa also grumbled if she touched the remote,

never mind the fact he started snoring two minutes after he sat down to watch television. Then there was the way he left his old man briefs, with shit stains that he claimed weren't his, on the floor of the bathroom. He didn't make for the best roommate, especially once her parents left.

Another pair of people she missed but didn't. While she loved Mom and Dad dearly, she'd been glad when they chose to spend most of their time elsewhere. Sometime in their late fifties, her parents suddenly decided they were nubile youngsters again. Chasing each other around. Giggling. Spending more time naked than clothed. Edwina might need therapy for the things she'd come across. It was a miracle she'd not gone blind.

A good thing she knew moms and dads didn't have sex. Edwina was immaculately conceived. What she saw? Surely a hallucination. Daddy merely spanked Mommy because she was bad.

Sob.

"It's been peaceful since Grandpa left." Too peaceful. It led to Edwina zoning out on the couch, partaking in a little too much of the sweet stuff and then lying there in a stupor. But in good news, she always got the remote.

"Where do I sign up?" Nexxie rubbed her hands in glee.

Laughter rumbled from Edwina. "It's easy. Just give your mom a ticket to go for a visit."

"What if she won't go?"

"Oh she will, because not only is she going to escape the bite-ass cold of winter, you're going to join her."

"Why would I do that?"

"To make sure she ends up in the right spot." In the case of her parents, Edwina dumped their necking butts at an adult community where some of their friends fled to in the winter. "And because once family gets a foothold down there, you know what that means for you?"

It took a moment, but eventually Nexxie's eyes widened. "I could go to PrideLand any time I wanted!"

PrideLand was a new theme park that not only offered roller coasters and other wild rides but it also had an animal reserve. For lions. A relaxing spa retreat for the animal lover.

"Don't say that name," Luna grumbled. "Joel is already threatening to make us do family road trips and embark on memory-making adventures when the baby is old enough."

"You can be the next Lionwald family." Nexxie clasped her hands. "I can't wait to see your antics on the big screen in the theater room."

"No one will be taping me." Luna glared at the younger girl. "I mean it."

"You say that now, but"—Nexxie cupped Luna's cheeks—"you're about to become a mom, and I have already wagered you'll be the type videotaping every single moment. Forcing us to watch it as you tell us about the big shit that almost went nuclear."

"Take that back!" Luna threatened, shaking her finger in Nexxie's face.

"Or what? You'll knock me down with that massive belly? You're being hormonal, preggo," Nexxie taunted, and Luna yelled, before lunging. Using evasive technique, the girl bolted with a waddling Luna on her tail, shaking her fist.

Edwina blinked. Bugging an about-to-pop Luna seemed a little much even for the lions.

Reba neared, shaking her head. "Poor Luna. She wants the baby out so badly. Last night she was eating food so spicy it's a wonder she's alive. Poor Joel was whining to all the boys about raw dick and something about her taking all the fun out of sex."

"Sex?" Edwina questioned. "I'm surprised she's in the mood."

"It's supposed to help induce labor. Today, she's exercising."

"Why bother with all that? She just needs some of my special honey 'O.'"

Reba frowned. "How will eating honey help?"

"She doesn't put it in her mouth," Edwina stated.

"Then where? On her belly?"

"Lower."

"Oh... *Oh.*" A cleared throat and a hesitant, "What does it do?"

"Intense orgasm. Enough to contract the uterus and get things going."

Reba stared at her. "Um, did you say orgasm?"

"Usually multiples."

"And does it work only on women?"

"Men too. It's very versatile." Edible and easy to wash off, it was an organic solution that not many knew about.

"I don't suppose you sell it?"

"As a matter of fact, I have a few small jars." She never had a large supply given the process involved in creating the specialized honey. Edwina quoted a price in the three digits, and the lioness didn't blink as she handed over her credit card. "I'll take one. Not for me," she hastened to add.

"Why not?"

"Because sex with my mate is already incredible."

"Think of it more as an enhancement."

Reba arched a brow. "You know what, make that two."

"I'll have it ready for when you leave, which you won't want to delay. There's a storm coming." It wouldn't be long before the bright sunshine turned to shadow. A dark cloud blotted the horizon. "Better grab an axe and get cutting."

"Stupid tradition. I don't see why we can't buy a tree from a lot," Reba grumbled.

"If you want to save yourself the hassle, I have

some precut," Edwina reminded, sweeping her hand to the left to show them off.

It led to pearly whites gleaming as a grinning Reba replied, "Okay, so I lied. I think we all love getting a chance to swing a blade."

"I know. And wait until you see the axes I special ordered for this season."

A squealed, "Oh my fucking god it's pink," had Reba's eyes widening.

"Hot damn. You didn't."

Edwina grinned. "I did. It was time we replaced the old stock, so I ordered some new ones. There's even a bedazzled blade." Edwina might run a tree and honey farm, but she knew her market. The lionesses' yearly Christmas tree hunt brought in the big bucks. The money laundering she did for the Pride kept her hobby farm more than afloat. She got a cut, they cleaned some dollars that they couldn't through their legit businesses, and everyone was happy.

"Don't tell my husband, but I think I love you." Reba hugged Edwina quickly before whirling to yell, "Touch the sparkly one and die, biatches!"

Someone hadn't changed.

Edwina hid a smile as Reba stalked off to get her sparkly axe.

Joan took her place. "Hello, gorgeous. I don't suppose you've turned bi since last year?" The athletic lioness offered a hopeful grin.

"What can I say? I'm still a lover of wood." Even if

the wood she'd been getting of late didn't really satisfy. At her ripe age of thirty-seven, she'd begun to wonder if she should think about widening her horizons.

"Shame. But you know where I am if you change your mind." Joan winked.

Edwina almost blushed. "How many trees do you need this year?"

"As many as we can load for the apartments, plus we'll need a beast for the lobby."

"I know just the one," Edwina said, only to blink as four people came trudging into the yard on foot. The twins, Teena and Meena, raced and tripped their way into the yard. Behind the twins was Melly, looking as bouncy and cheerful as usual but accompanying her was an oddly dressed person. They wore sunglasses, a fancy wide-brimmed hat, a long navy-blue pea coat, boots that wouldn't survive even an inch of snow, and gloves that probably made the cold worse. "Who the fuck is that?"

Joan smirked. "Arik's cousin, Felix. Some kind of prince from overseas. Arrived yesterday. He heard we were going tree picking and insisted on helping, which I couldn't blame him for, given his other choice was going to a kids' play place with Arik because his boy got invited to a party. I'd rather go tree cutting too."

Edwina cast him a doubtful glance as he moved warily over the rutted ice and slush. "I don't think he'll be much use looking like that."

"As if we need him or any man to cut wood. Like,

hello, I've been handling wood for a long time," Reba purred with innuendo as she returned with her sparkly axe. She swung it and let the rhinestones catch the light.

"He's going to freeze in those clothes," Edwina muttered.

"If it's any consolation, under that crap, he's actually quite pretty." He must be since Joan was the one to make the remark.

Edwina wrinkled her nose. "I'll take useful over pretty, thank you."

"Speaking of pretty..." Joan drawled.

Edwina grinned. "I didn't forget. I just didn't put your new ax with the others. Yours is by the door to my house." An ax that Joan special ordered and had sent as a gift with just one caveat, *Mine during our tree day*.

The axe, custom crafted by a metal smith, used a secret alloy that ensured the blade never rusted or dulled. It could cut through anything with a powerful stroke. Edwina had been waiting for Joan to get the first swing in since she bought it before using it herself.

As Reba and Joan moved off, Melly took their place.

"Can I borrow your phone? Mine's fried." Melly shook her cell in her direction. "I need to call a tow truck. Our ride died a mile down the road. Like something zapped it. All the electronics, including our phones, went dead."

That arched her brow. "How the hell did you manage that?"

Melly shrugged. "Blame his highness spritzing himself. I think he might have misted the electrical. Then had the nerve to complain because we had to walk the rest of the way in. Wait until he finds out he'll have to bum a ride with someone else on the way back and get squished." She snickered.

"Use my phone," Edwina offered, holding out her cell, already unlocked.

"Thanks." As Melly moved off to order a tow, the prince worked his way over to her, looking ridiculous up close and smelling of lotion. Little of his face could be seen given the oversized lenses, hat pulled low, and collar turned up.

"My lady." He sketched a partial bow.

She arched a brow. "Can I help you?"

"I am Felix Charlemagne, cousin to Arik, visiting for the holidays."

"Good for you."

"We require some trees."

"And?"

"Aren't you the vendor?" he drawled. "Show me your wares."

Imperious prick. She pointed. "Over there are some precuts."

He glanced. "I don't think that's enough."

"It's not."

"Well?"

"Well, what?"

"We need more trees."

"I know. And so do they." Edwina gestured to the women moving off into the grove. "What do think they have the axes for?"

He turned to eye the lionesses wandering the neat rows of trees.

"Fantastic. Fresh cut. Marvelous idea, but I'm afraid I'm not quite dressed for traipsing in the woods."

"You're right. You're not." At least he recognized it. Perhaps he'd even done it on perhaps so he wouldn't have to exert himself.

"It's cold. I don't suppose you have an office where I can warm up?"

"Nope."

"What about a store? I hear you also sell honey."

"I do sell honey, but I don't have a store," she replied as she walked away, heading for the tree part of her farm.

He tagged along. "Word is your honey has remarkable traits."

"If you say so." She knew better than to say too much to a stranger.

"My mother was saying I should buy some."

"Then maybe you should."

"Since you don't have a store, do you have a website? I tried looking you up but didn't find anything other than a business listing for Honey Pine Farm."

"Don't need a website or store."

To his credit, while she could hear annoyance brimming in his tone, his face remained smooth. "How are you supposed to attract buyers?"

"I have enough clients." She sold her stuff via special order.

"What if I want to buy some?"

"I'll think about it."

As his jaw dropped, she turned from the prince and walked away. She snared a rope for her sledge, bright red and parked on the front lawn. When they had horses, they used to pull it. Now Edwina wrapped the rope tether around her upper body. At least it was light and the runners would slide on the icy tracks.

"Where are you going with that?" his royal pain in the ass asked as she trudged past some of the Pride ladies cutting down some of the simple trees for household use. Edwina signaled to Reba, who'd gleefully used her shiny new sharp weapon to timber a six-footer.

"You coming to get the big one?" Edwina hollered.

"Hell yeah." Reba grabbed hold of Joan and joined Edwina. Between the three of them, they should be enough to haul a big one back, because she doubted the tag-along prince would be much use. Thus far, he'd only been good at running his mouth.

"Are we going far?" he asked, following behind the sled while Reba and Joan went ahead to scout the prospects.

"Yup." The older parts of her forest would be where they'd find a specimen large enough to satisfy.

"Will it take long? The weather looks to be getting rough."

"Yup." Then she repeated, "Storm is coming."

"Is it wise to continue?" The prince just didn't stop with his nattering.

"If you're scared, you can turn around."

"Not scared," he grumbled. "Just using common sense. People get lost in storms."

"Fear not, prince, you'll be fine, or are you worried you'll get snow in your hair?" she mocked.

"More like wondering if I'll get frostbite. No one warned me it would be this cold."

"It's winter."

"I hadn't noticed," he replied sarcastically.

"Why are you here if this isn't your cup of honey?"

"Because it sounded interesting. Go pick a tree. Try this honey I've been hearing about. Decorate while sipping some creamy nog."

"If this is too much for your little pampered feet, you could always go back to the farm and wait."

"My feet aren't little."

"Pity your ego isn't."

"Nothing wrong with being confident," he stated, pulling off his glasses as it began to get dark in the forest.

Joan was right. He was pretty.

But still not her type. "Are you visiting for long?"

"Depends on how my business goes. Arik and I are looking to merge our talents to create new products. Would something like that interest you with your honey?"

"No."

"You haven't even let me pitch a suggestion."

"Because I'm not interested. I've got enough work as is without getting involved with some snooty royals to make overpriced crap."

"Charlemagne perfumes and lotions are high-end products."

"Good for you."

"You're very stubborn."

She paused to arch a brow at him. "Thank you." She continued to trudge, and he sighed.

"Is it much longer? My feet are frozen."

"And not likely to get any better, as we're not there yet. Once we are, we have to cut the tree down, load it, and bring it back."

He eyed his feet. His boots were rigid leather that probably didn't stop the cold or wet. "I think it might be best if I turn around."

"Buh-by," she muttered and then paid him no mind as she followed the sounds of laughter and thunking as an axe met a tree trunk.

She found Reba and Joan taking turns cutting down a nice twelve-footer. While they worked quickly, chipping at the wood, she readied the sledge for loading. She didn't want to waste time once it fell. It had gotten much darker since she set out, the storm moving in quicker than expected. They'd have to hurry back. She wouldn't want anyone to be caught outside when the storm hit.

"Timber!" Reba yelled as the tree came down and caused snow to briefly hang in the air.

They quickly strapped it to the sledge, and then the three women began to pull their prize back, singing off-key.

"Oh Christmas tree, oh Christmas tree,
"How lovely you are for scratching!
"Oh Christmas Tree, Oh Christmas Tree,
"You'll make a great perch for napping."

CHAPTER THREE

ON THE EVE OF THE FOURTH DAY OF CHRISTMAS, A GROUCHY BEAR GAVE TO ME— NOTHING. NOT EVEN ANY RESPECT FOR THE MANE.

The weather turned quickly, and if Felix thought he'd shivered when he got out of the warm SUV after it stalled, it was nothing compared to now. Fucking frigid. Why would anyone choose to live here? And what was the weather doing to his hair?

He tromped the path back to the farm, wishing his mother had sent him somewhere warm to do business. Although the real mistake came in volunteering to help with the tree picking. In his defense, he assumed it would be easy. Go to tree farm. Point at tree. Take tree home.

Not even close. The enthusiasm with which the lionesses wielded those axes caused a moment of worry. One wrong swing...

Rather than play dodge the enthusiastic blades, he'd chosen to stick close to the farm owner. One Edwina Barkley. American brown bear shifter, late twenties judging by her unwrinkled skin. She not only owned the farm but she ran it almost entirely alone.

A woman to admire, and she'd looked at Felix and pegged him as a spoiled royal. Not entirely wrong. It suited Felix for people to underestimate him. Yes, he put great stock in his appearance, but that didn't make him useless or dumb.

But she'd not looked past his appearance before dismissing him as unworthy, whereas he'd gazed upon her and seen a woman of strength. And in that solid nature, he also saw her beauty. Like many of her kind she had wide hips and a generous chest. Voluptuous but not fat. Big boned and strong. Healthy looking in body, but he couldn't tell a thing about her hair pulled back in tight French braids. He did know she stood eye to eye with him.

And not once had she looked back when he declared he was turning around. He knew because he'd kept peeking.

Alone, he'd trudged back in the direction they'd come, or so he assumed. The sharp air did much to kill scent, as did the lotion he'd lathered to protect his skin from chapping.

A flicker of red off the beaten path caught the corner of his eye. Probably one of the females of Arik's Pride toying with him. They'd chosen their name well. Biatches. They epitomized the term bratty. He could probably expect a snowball to the head or even a pounce from above. They'd done it to him once already today.

At the condo, he'd chosen to take the stairs to avoid the crowded elevator, only to have his hair messed up as a lioness went sliding down the rail, flicking his tresses as she whipped by. A good thing he kept an emergency comb in his pocket.

A light flutter of snowflakes drew his attention to the fact the clouds had moved in and begun dumping their contents. It meant he had no sun to direct him, nor even GPS to guide hi since his phone had died when the SUV did, part of the mysterious electrical failure. Surely it was only a coincidence that when he spritzed his skin with a protectant that was still in beta, that everything suddenly buzzed and died. Perhaps he should study it a bit further before approving it for mass production.

The woods appeared deeper and darker than he recalled coming in. It made the brief glimpses of red he spotted stark. Someone shadowed him. Had his cousin set one of the lionesses as a guard? Or could this be something more nefarious? After all, the Charlemagne family did have wealth and clout.

Felix ducked behind a tree and then proceeded to zigzag among them as the falling snow thickened. How long since he'd left Edwina? How far still from the farm?

Under the boughs of a massive tree with a fat trunk, he stood for a moment, listening and doing his best to conceal his frosty breath. The snow fell thickly, covering his tracks, causing concern. What if he needed to retrace his steps?

Thunk.

Something fell and bounced off his head. He rubbed the crown and glanced up. Just in time to get a face full of snow.

The shock of cold had him gasping and yelling. "Argh. Ugh. Ick." He admittedly wasn't a winter kind of guy.

A more cautious peek overhead showed more snow waiting to fall. On purpose, he realized, catching a hint of red. Aha. Now he had his stalker.

He jumped at the lowest branch on the tree and heard it creak. Not that he paid it much mind given more of the cold stuff hit him. He shook his head, flinging snow and slush, and eyed the many branches above. Still thick with needles, the many crisscrossing branches formed a web that captured snow and hid the culprit.

Felix might be a prince, but he was a fit one. He pulled himself onto the first fat branch. More snow fell from above, and while he did his best to dodge by canting his head, some still managed to get into that space between his neck and jacket. Cold. So cold on his skin.

A rustle of branches as something moved through them had him shouting, "Who's there? Did my cousin send you?" With the deepening gloom, he couldn't see much.

Creak. Crack. The reply to his query came as proof that someone shared the tree. A biatch was obviously screwing with him.

Not very welcoming. A prince should be coddled by the fire and fed, not shivering in the cold and taunted.

He lowered himself from the tree and huffed, "You've had your measure of entertainment. Time to get back to the farm."

The branches quivered before they dumped more snow.

This time he managed to stay dry. Ha. He planted his hands on his hips. "Enough of your winter games. Show yourself."

He didn't expect his demand to actually work, only, to his surprise, despite the deepening gloom, he caught a hint of movement then something red.

A scarlet hat with a white pompom tip appeared before the squirrel wearing it did, a big brown specimen with a massive bushy tail. Unexpected and, at the same time, a squirrel couldn't have been what stalked him. It had to be something bigger. Fiercer. "Who's your accomplice? Who are you working for?"

The squirrel chirped something that even to his untrained ear probably was rude.

It was too much. First the lack of respect from his cousin's Pride and now this rodent?

"Don't you give me any lip, squirrel. I've had enough of the boorish manners of Americans." He shook his fist as emphasis, and his speech caught the red-hatted squirrel's attention. It cocked its head and stared down at him, its paws hugging something tight to its body.

"What's that you've got?"

The squirrel turned with its prize.

"I asked what you were hiding." Because now that his feline curiosity had been aroused, he had to know. Felix jumped to grab the branch it sat on. His fingers gripped bark, but before he could hoist himself, the squirrel tilted its head, appeared to shrug, and extended it paws, dropping the acorn it had been hugging. It fell and smacked Felix right between his eyes.

He blinked. It hadn't hurt, but the squirrel holding its belly as if it laughed? That stung.

Cr-a-a-ack.

His eyes barely had time to widen as the massive conifer began to lean. The squirrel leapt as Felix let go of the branch. He hit the ground below but didn't move fast enough to avoid the tree.

It slammed him, face first, into the snow.

CHAPTER FOUR

HARK THE ANGELIC BIATCHES SING, GLORY TO OUR LION KING.

The raucous singing kept the biatches warm amidst the falling snow as they emerged from the forest and orchards, dragging their prizes. Not the bodies of their enemies—because Arik, being a spoilsport, said they couldn't—but the trees they'd conquered.

With the flakes falling thickly and the sky a dark stormy color that spoke of hours of snow to come, the lionesses quickly lashed them to the beds of trucks and onto the roof racks of the other vehicles, a mound of greenery quickly turning white. It led to the women leaving in haste, many not in the same ride as they'd arrived in. A few more crowded, given Melly's ride had died on the way in. They waved goodbye to Edwina, some of them hugging paper bags with stashes of honey inside. While Edwina had only a few jars of Honey

"O," she did have honey lotion, honey candy, and honey-bee-calm.

The trip back to the city took a bit longer than usual due to the road conditions. After being cooped up for too long, they arrived and tumbled out of the vehicles with great chaos, which increased as the males joined them to flex muscle carrying trees inside. The biatches allowed it mostly so the stack of pizzas in the lobby didn't go cold.

After they'd mowed down all the slices, most lingered as the public tree was put in its brace and lights were wound around it.

Children decorated the lower branches, leaving the majority of the higher branches bare. Once the kiddoes went to bed, the adults would redistribute the ornaments while downing shots of fireball, sipping eggnog, and singing bawdy Christmas songs.

"Hey, where's his royal vainness?" asked Nexxie while eating popcorn instead of stringing it for the tree.

"Wasn't he with Melly?" Luna turned from the tree, her belly knocking off a few balls. The betting pool was getting tighter the further she went past her due date. Whoever won the pot of money would be rolling in green.

Melly shook her head. "Not with me. My SUV died, so I snagged a ride with Joan."

"Who did he ride with then?" Reba asked. When no one answered, she huffed, "Come on, easy question.

It's not like you wouldn't have noticed him. The man never shuts up about hair and skin."

The biatches shared glances and got caught by Leo passing through. He halted, shook his head, and made it halfway to the door before flipping around and stalking toward those gathered growling, "What did you do now?"

"There's a teensy tiny chance we lost Arik's cousin." Melly squished her fingers almost together.

"Felix is missing, and you just noticed? How many hours later?" The quieter he got the more they hung their heads. Leo crossed arms over his very wide chest. "Someone needs to tell Arik. He thought his cousin was having so much fun he forgot their dinner plans." Leo arched a brow. "Anyone?"

Contrite expressions abounded. Leo might not be Alpha, but he was Omega for a reason.

"We'll find him," Reba promised.

"Damned straight you will. When did you last see him?"

"He rode with me to the tree farm," Melly volunteered. "But we split up once we got there."

"And when you left, no one noticed he was missing?"

Again, glances were exchanged, and much shrugging ensued as they realized no one had seen him during the packing-up-and-moving-out phase.

"You forgot the king's cousin, a visiting prince, at

the tree farm?" Leo's low rumble suddenly resulted in Meena appearing, throwing herself at her mate.

"Don't kill them, pookie!"

"They lost Felix," he growled, using just one arm to support the curvy weight of his wife.

"And they feel awful. They are totally going to find him, right, biatches?" Meena practically spun her head as she hissed out the last part. "Because if my husband has to go out tonight hunting down the prince, after I managed to finagle my kids sleeping over at Auntie Nora's, there will be hell to pay." Meena's glare indicated that hell would hurt.

"I'll go get him!" Nexxie announced, bouncing from the couch and falling over.

"Me too!" Joan volunteered, sloshing her spiked eggnog.

"You've all had too much to drink. Especially considering the storm outside." Leo's observation reminded them of the whipping winds and snows. They'd blocked out the ugly weather when they'd closed the security shutters for the night.

"If he's still at the farm, then how come Edwina didn't call to tell us?" Luna mused aloud.

"Storm probably blocked her signal. And she couldn't drive since the roads are shut down," Melly surmised.

"Out there in the boonies, I'll bet the power went out." Nexxie's addition.

"They're most likely snuggling for warmth," Meena chimed in.

"Naked," was the next wicked addition.

All eyes rounded as they gasped, "Auntie Maeve!" Auntie Maeve had just celebrated ninety-eight.

"They'll be snowed in for days, a prince lion and a farmer bear, who will fall madly in love and get married on Christmas." Meena clasped her hands and sighed.

Silence followed. Then raucous laughter—*"Edwina is too smart to fall for a pampered prince." "Pretty sure she swings for my team even if she won't go out for a drink." "Can't see it. She'd break him."*

Leo growled. "This is not a Christmas romance. Arik's cousin is missing. What are we going to do about it?"

"Nothing," Luna declared.

"What do you mean, nothing?" Leo ogled them. "You're the Pride biatches. Our huntresses."

"Yeah, but it's snowing." Said with a duh overtone.

Heads nodded all around.

And Leo sighed as he finally remembered lions didn't do snow.

But bears did.

CHAPTER FIVE

ON THE NEVER-ENDING THIRD DAY OF BEARMAS, A CLIENT GAVE TO ME – A REASON TO GET AN UNLISTED NUMBER.

The phone rang, and Edwina almost ignored it. Her chair was much too comfortable. Her blanket was positioned just right. But then she remembered the honey cookies she'd forgotten and a cup of honeyed milk to wash them down. As she ran for the kitchen, suddenly in dire need of a snack, she snared her phone in passing and answered.

"Honey Pine Farm, we're closed until the roads are cleared." Might as well get that part out of the way since they'd entered the desperate week before Christmas when people who'd waited too long for a tree would pay anything. This was also the week of excuses when people showed up. *Our dog ate the tree we had. The cat destroyed the tree. My ex-boyfriend stole the tree. I never get any time off. I don't believe in Christmas.* And then there was the, *What's your return policy?*

"Edwina, it's Melly."

"Hey," she muttered as she eyed the cookie tin and the honey jar on the counter. A premonition had her snaring the latter, and she toted it back to her comfy chair.

"So this is probably a crazy question—I mean, obviously, he's there with you—but like, we kind of need to confirm because, you know, he's the king's cousin, and like, well, there's a little worry he might be upset, but in my defense, I thought he was someone else's problem, only it turns out, none of us were watching—"

Edwina interrupted. "For honey's sake, what are you prattling about?"

"The prince. He's with you at the farm."

"No." And as Edwina said it, before Melly could say another word, she knew. "He's missing, isn't he?"

"Yeah." Melly's voice got small. "And boy is the king pissed."

Which wasn't actually Edwina's problem. However, these were her very best clients, and everyone knew lions didn't do snow. Especially blizzards.

Sigh.

"I'll go find him," she offered reluctantly.

"Oh, you are the very best bear ever. We are going to totally owe you for this."

"Whatever." Edwina hung up the phone and didn't crush it. Great control on her part given she was mightily tempted. Instead, she ate her emotions, dabbing a huge dipper into her pot of honey, swirling, and then sucking it clean. Savoring the sweetness.

Mmm.

Delicious.

Especially this version, the nectar created from the bees collecting pollen from specially grown jasmine flowers. Known for its calming nature, the special blend, with a hint of peppermint, helped tone down her annoyance at the fact she had to go out in the nasty storm looking for an idiot instead of watching *Yellowstone*, her absolute favorite show. It lacked bears, but Beth made up for it.

Rather than cheer on the saucy ranch heiress, Edwina stripped and flipped into her shaggy bear fur before lumbering out into the storm, looking for a prince. Partially her own fault. She'd not even realized the idiot was missing. She'd been too busy getting the trees lashed and keeping the rambunctious lionesses from swinging axes at each other. And before you thought they'd be smart enough to be careful, think again.

As a young girl, Edwina had witnessed firsthand what could happen when the rowdy ones were left unchecked. Like literally seen a lioness of the time swing her axe a little too hard and sever the toes from her foot.

What did Grandpa do as little Edwina gaped in horror at the pooling blood? He lifted the cut section of shoe with the toes inside and, rather than put them on ice and rush the owner to the hospital to sew them back on, boomed, "These will be delicious deep fried." With that announcement, he stomped into the house.

The lioness, who'd accidentally chopped off a part of her own body, hobbled off without argument, and the following year, and the year after, there were no accidents.

But that happened a lifetime ago. These newer felines needed to perhaps have a mishap of their own to learn. Would Edwina have to eat someone to make a point? Last time she'd been too leery to have a taste. But lion toes sure smelled good when deep fried then drizzled with a bit of honey and salt.

How would an entire lion taste roasted? She might soon find out, because five minutes into the storm and she doubted the idiot prince would survive. The wind whipped something cold and fierce, even for someone like her. The snow fell in thick flakes. Bearable for someone with thick fur or the proper outer garments, but he'd not been dressed at all for the weather, and switching into his lion with thin fur wouldn't improve that situation.

So why was she bothering looking for a pop-si-lion? Because maybe, just maybe, he was tougher than he looked. But an idiot since he'd obviously gotten lost. Although how had he managed that? He only had to follow the path, which led right back to the farm, unless... There was that one fork. Just the single tiny one. Surely he'd taken the left.

Hmm. Maybe she should have mentioned it. Or maybe he shouldn't have been an annoying twat and either stuck close to Edwina or stayed at the farm in the first place.

Argh. It made her wish she'd chosen to migrate south earlier than planned. Some might wonder that she didn't hunker and hibernate. Those people didn't spend all spring working off those extra pounds.

Having a vague idea of where he might have gotten lost, she headed in that direction, hoping for a clue since she had no trail to sniff out. The storm had spent the last few hours covering everything in a layer of snow a few inches deep.

Her breath frosted as she slowed and lumbered her way through fluffy drifts, making sure to sniff side to side. She had no light to see by. With night fallen, and the blizzard-like conditions, she relied on other senses. Listening. Smelling. Mostly she trusted her instinct—fueled with a little honey. Don't scoff. Just ask Winnie the Pooh. Honey made the world a much better place.

Knowing these woods as well as she did, she let impulse guide her, and it led her to the older parts of the forest with the true giants—a logger's wet dream. She'd had many offers to buy this section, given it didn't just have conifers too big for use but the ever-popular birch.

Having grown up in these woods, she knew every inch. Every tree. Enough to realize in her almost blind search that one had fallen. She nosed around its stump and discovered a jagged wound in the wood. It had split and recently, judging by the freshness.

She lumbered around the fallen tree, nosing under the branches. Many of them were snapped by the impact, but some of the older ones had a thick enough base that the bulk of the tree remained lifted from the ground, forming pockets where a man could survive, sheltered.

Toward the far edge, almost impaled and smothered in boughs that insulated from the cold, she found the prince.

She grunted, but he didn't reply. His shallow breathing most likely indicated unconsciousness. She'd have to remove him to assess any damage.

She cracked a few branches enough to ram her upper body inside. She clamped onto his coat and heaved. He didn't whine. A good thing or she'd have knocked him out. She wasn't about to start listening to him complain.

Once she'd cleared him of the tree, she gave him the once-over, sniffing him. Blood on his face from a cut already scabbing over. Not unexpected since he'd been knocked out. Hard apparently, given how long he'd been lying there. A lick to his face let her check his temperature. Cool but not hypothermic. Tastier than expected. She flicked him again just for fun.

His eyes opened, and he stared at her, his eyes unfocussed.

She didn't move lest he freak out. That happened

once in high school. She'd finally slept with her boyfriend, Kendrick, and to celebrate, they got drunk. She got a little too relaxed and flipped shapes while passed out. An equally wasted Kendrick woke, saw her furry shape, and screamed, "Bear attack!" Since she didn't want her daddy to hear and kill Kendrick for deflowering his cub, and still a little drunk, she might have swung Kendrick a few times against a tree to make him shut up. Kendrick, a hyena who should have known better in the first place, broke up with her once he left the hospital. Ended up changing schools to avoid her.

Felix blinked in her direction, only the whites of his eyes gleaming, and slurred, "I don't have a picnic basket."

She almost ate him at the insult. As if ursine took after that silly Yogi bear. Picnic baskets usually had sandwiches and fruits. A smart bear went after the coolers with burgers, dogs, and beer.

His eyes shut and remained shut. The prince didn't wake as she dragged his limp butt all the way home and this despite the fact his hair got snagged a few times. His fault. If he was gonna have long locks, then he should have braided it before traipsing in the woods. At least he didn't wear it in a bun. Or did he? Edwina couldn't stand the new manbun trend. She had been raised as a feminist and sexist all at once, confident and take charge, but at the same time she liked a man who oozed masculinity. It annoyed that because of her brash nature and, as some people delicately put—even as it was anything but delicate—big-boned body type, she attracted those looking to be submissive in a relationship. Even guys bigger than her never saw her as delicate or worthy of the niceties the more petite enjoyed.

She doubted the prince, of a size with her, would be any different. Not that it mattered. For one, he wasn't her type. Edwina never dated men with hair past their shoulders because Grandpa always warned her to stay away from long-haired hippies. But he'd not said much about princes.

When she arrived at her cabin, she dragged the prince in and slammed the door shut against the storm. Just that brief opening had sent in a draft and a dusting of snow. The power had predictably gone out, but she had no need for the generator yet. The fire in her fat-bellied stove remained strong and pushed out plenty of heat.

Leaving the limp prince in a heap on the floor, she headed for that warmth, shaking her snowy fur as she passed him, shifting as she went, until she got close enough to feel the heat on her belly and breasts.

Ah. So nice. She warmed her front before whirling to roast her naked butt. She shook all her limbs, negating the cold, jiggling and wiggling to remove the chill. The prince of course chose that moment to wake.

He rolled over and fluttered ridiculously wasted lashes in her direction. "Holy mother of god. I've died and gone to heaven. Are you my reward for being a good kitty?"

The unexpected compliment flustered. Edwina walked to the blanket hung over her chair and tossed a nonchalant reply. "You should be so lucky. How are you feeling?"

"Cold."

"Not surprising given how I found you."

"What happened?" He sat up and rubbed a hand over his face.

"You managed to be under a tree when it fell."

"Seriously?" He gaped at her for a minute.

"Very." She approached and dropped to her haunches. "So let me ask you again, how are you feeling?"

He blinked at her. "Fine, but, uh, why are you naked?"

"Because someone had to go find you in the blizzard."

"Um. That doesn't make sense." His forehead creased. "It's too cold to be without clothing outside."

"I was in my bear fur. Plenty warm, unlike you in your trendy, but useless gear, prince."

"You wear fur? Isn't that like murder?" His eyes widened, and it occurred to her he really had no idea what she meant when she claimed to wear fur. Was it possible to get hit hard enough he didn't remember they were shifters? She'd never heard of such a thing.

Her turn to stare at him. "You'd better not be screwing with me, prince."

"Is that my name?"

She touched his head, careful of the scratch on his temple thinly scabbed, not showing red signs of infection. He also had a pale bruise between the eyes. "You're not feverish. Any pain?"

"Just a bit of a headache."

"Probably from when the tree fell on you."

"So you keep saying. I don't remember."

"What's the last thing you recall?"

He stared at her. Opened and shut his mouth a few times before saying, "Nothing."

"It appears the blow to your head has taken away your memory of the accident."

"Not just the accident. Where am I? Who are you?"

Her lips flattened, and she muttered, "You just couldn't stick to the path. Idiot!"

"Why are you mad at me?"

"Because I didn't want to be dealing with an amnesiac tonight. I had better things to do."

"Like?"

"Like watch *Yellowstone*. Hell, I'd rather sort my lonely sock drawer than be here talking to you." She couldn't help but scowl.

His turn to press his lips tight. "Well, excuse me for not understanding what's going on. It's not as if I don't have a head wound, which is obviously causing some cognition difficulties."

"Bah. You've got sort term memory loss. Give it a few hours, you'll be fine."

"What if I'm not? I should be in a hospital."

"Don't be silly. Even if the roads weren't impassable, there isn't anything they could do for you."

"You don't know that for sure. Maybe they have some medicine or tricks to help me remember."

"I'm sure you've not forgotten anything important."

"I don't even remember my name," he complained.

"I can help you there. Name is Simba." She did her best to conceal her mirth. If she had to be stuck with an annoying prince, might as well have some fun.

"Simba?" Both his brows lifted. "Are you sure?"

"Very."

"It doesn't feel right."

"That's because you hate it."

"Earlier, you called me prince. Am I royalty?"

She shook her head. "It's your middle name. Your mother loved his singing." When he appeared to not comprehend, she sang a few lines from "Raspberry Beret" and "When Doves Cry."

"This is all so strange." He rubbed his face. "Where am I?" He glanced around, and she knew what he'd see: a large cabin. Although some might call it a lodge, given it had two bedrooms on the main level and a loft that provided a third and overlooked a massive great room. Pine cabinets painted a bright blue lined an entire wall, the countertop made of concrete. The island, though, had a butcher block.

"We're home," Edwina stated, and since she didn't clarify her home, he misconstrued.

"I live here?" He sounded so surprised. Before she could correct him, she almost choked because he added, "Are we a couple?"

She almost exclaimed no. As if she'd ever date someone like him. However, his gaze had returned to her boobs. The blanket tucked over hid them, but a chesty girl, she still had cleavage. The longer he looked, the warmer the feeling between her legs got.

She could tell the truth, but... Messing with him would be much more fun.

"We are more than just a couple, my silly prince. We're married."

"Married?" He rose to his feet, of a height with her, but indoors he appeared wider than she recalled. Probably mostly bulky from his coat. He looked the type to have shoulder pads sewn in.

"More than ten years now, my big hunk of hot honey." She simpered, batting her lashes, probably doing it wrong, but she couldn't stop herself now.

"Married? You don't wear a ring." He eyed her hand.

"Because I don't want to wreck it when I work. Not to mention, what if it got lost? It's so precious to me."

He remained skeptical, and it bugged her that yet

another man didn't see her as bride material. She stalked to the bedroom that belonged to her parents. Her mother's jewelry box remained with a few pieces Edwina would inherit. Including Grandma's ring.

She returned with it, feeling odd with it sitting on her left hand. She held it out. "Happy now, husband?"

"I guess. Yeah." He peeled off his gloves and placed them on a bench by the front door. His jacket followed, the fabric not at all bulky. A bigger man emerged than expected. Not bear thick, like her dad and grandpa, but not shabby either. He grimaced at his boots.

"These are pretty useless," he stated.

"I told you so when you bought them, but you just wouldn't listen. The chore of being married to a fashionable man."

"Remind me to never wear them again." He kicked them off and stood in his socks. "They're wet, too. Where do I keep my dry ones?"

It hit her that the lie would unravel since he didn't actually have any clothes here. But her family did. "Hold on, I'll get them for you."

She dashed into Grandpa's room and dug through his drawer, pulled out dry socks. Couldn't bring herself to take underwear, although she did snare a plain cable-knit sweater and soft plaid sleep pants. She brought the garments out to the prince, who stood in front of the fire, holding out his hands to warm them.

"Why was I outside?" he asked as she came level with him.

"Being a traditionalist, you wanted to find me the perfect tree." She handed him the clothes.

"In a storm?"

"It hit suddenly."

He pulled the sweater on. "How did you find me?" He stared at her as if interrogating, and she had to think quick. If he didn't remember he could shift, then she needed a more logical explanation.

"I tracked your phone." And then so he wouldn't think her a stalker, laughed and added, "I thought you were crazy for making me install the app, but look at that, it helped save you."

"You brought me back by yourself?" He glanced down at his pants then her, as if uncertain.

She almost turned away when he tugged the slim-fitting trousers down, but a married wife wouldn't, so she remained facing him, doing her best to not peek and see if he wore briefs or shorts. Did his package show?

"I had the pull-along sled with me." Another lie. But in for an ounce of honey, in for the whole pound.

"Are you telling me you dragged me home all by yourself?" Incredulity had him pausing with the sleep pants pulled up only to his knees. Her quick glance showed tight black underpants outlining what surely had to be a pair of socks.

She gave a high laugh as she replied, "Do you see anyone else around?"

"My poor wife. You must be exhausted." His

sudden solicitude had her eyes widening. He finished dressing and pushed her into a chair. "Sit. Rest."

"I'm fine."

"Nonsense. I am not a small man. The strain must have been incredible. Not to mention the cold." He hit the floor and grabbed her feet, the impromptu massage drawing a groan.

"It was pretty chilly," she agreed. "Hence why I stripped the moment I got home. If you'd not woken up, my next step was to get you naked for a snuggle to warm you up."

He paused his massage. "I am still feeling a tad chilled. Perhaps we should."

No surprise, the man might not remember his name, but his libido had no problem with recalling how to be a perv. "Now, now, my prince. I know that salacious look in your eye, and yes, I am as eager as you to reconnect bodily and affirm our loving married bond, but I already almost lost you once today, and given your, um, weak heart, it wouldn't do to have you overindulge while recovering from your ordeal. Trust me when I say I am as bereft as you about the situation."

"Oh." He appeared at a loss for words.

She pointed to the empty recliner by her side. "You should have a seat before you keel over." Or make her come just kneading her toes. The man had magic hands.

He plunked into the chair and reclined far enough

his feet could cook by the stove. He sighed. "This is nice."

"It is," she agreed, although there were times it could be lonely. Not by choice. Edwina would love nothing more than to have a companion by her side on the long winter nights. Alas, she'd yet to meet her own bear charming.

"Thank you for saving me," he said of a sudden.

"Anytime, *husband*."

"What happened to calling me prince?"

"Prince. Husband. Lover…" She batted her lashes. "Pity you're hurt, or I know how I'd remind you of our special bond."

"Not that hurt." He waggled his brows and offered her a rakish grin.

She almost took him up on the offer but didn't want to deal with his regret when he came to his senses.

"Now isn't the time, my prince. You need to heal. Get some sleep and we'll see how you feel in the morning."

"Is it safe to sleep? I thought people with concussions were supposed to remain awake."

"Er, yes, you're right. I will set an alarm to wake you at intervals."

"How? The power is out."

He might not remember his name, but his power of observation remained sharp even in a strange place.

"My watch has plenty of battery. I'm surprised you noticed."

"Nothing is humming, and your internet router by the television is dead."

"Don't worry. It happens all the time. We'll be fine. I've got enough wood inside for us to stay warm."

"Are you sure? I could fetch some more," he offered.

"I think you've gotten lost enough for one day. You should go to bed. It'll be a long day digging out tomorrow."

"Okay." He glanced around. "Stupid question, but where is my bed?"

She stood and pointed to her grandfather's room where she'd gotten the clothes. "You sleep in there. Two-piece bathroom is through the wooden door beside the bifold closet."

He spilled out of the recliner to stand a little too close. "You make it sound like we don't sleep together."

"Because we don't." Then, since he'd probably ask, she gave him a good excuse. "I snore. Loudly, like a bear."

"Oh."

"Yeah. You hate it and banished me to another room."

"Wait, I kicked you out of our bed?"

"Yes, but don't worry about it. It was a total marriage saver."

"But—"

She cut him off. "No butts for you tonight! Get some rest."

"Fine. Good night..." He paused. "I feel stupid for even asking, but what is your name?"

"Edwina."

"Edwina," he said musingly. "That's a lot of syllables. I doubt I use them all. What's my pet name for you?"

"Uh, uh—" Her mind blanked.

He was the one to say, "Honeybear. Your nickname is Honeybear. I remember."

Highly doubtful. No one ever dared call her that. Nor did she point out Honeybear had as many syllables as Edwina. Not with that smile on his face. Instead, she said softly, "See you in the morning."

The kiss he planted on her mouth was unexpected, as was the fact she didn't cuff him for it. He didn't try to take advantage and murmured, "Night, my sweet Honeybear," before heading to Grandpa's room.

She went to bed thinking maybe he wasn't so bad.

She woke to him at the foot of her bed, blustering, "Simba?"

CHAPTER SIX

ON THE FOURTH DAY OF CHRISTMAS, MY HOSTESS GAVE TO ME—OLD MAN CLOTHES AND DAMN HER IF THEY WEREN'T COMFORTABLE.

"I see you got your memories back," the reply Felix got when he confronted Edwina about her trick.

"Do I look like a Simba?" he hissed, still offended.

"Wailing male cub? Check." She rolled out of the bed, still naked. Did the woman not own any clothes?

He glanced away from her. "You lied to me."

"Played a prank, which I knew wouldn't last long. Don't be such a pussy about it. It was funny."

To her maybe, but he'd gone to sleep lusting after the woman he thought was his wife, only to wake horny with the realization he could do nothing about it.

"Not amused." He grimaced but only for a moment. Didn't want to give any ideas to lurking wrinkles.

"What's wrong, Simba? Didn't get your beauty rest?"

"I rested fine. Although my skin could use some

moisturizer considering you sent me to bed without any and after the day I had."

She blinked. "Do you seriously put on lotion every night?"

"How do you think my skin remains so supple?" He angled his head to show off the smooth column of his throat.

"Sounds like a lot of work."

"The alternative is aging prematurely and scaly flesh."

"If you say so."

"You'll understand when you get to be my age."

"Which is?"

"Thirty-five."

She snorted.

"What's so funny?"

"The fact I'm older than you by two years."

"You are not."

"Not sure why I'd lie about my age." She turned and headed for a wardrobe, her rounded ass wiggling with each step.

The lion in him wanted to pounce and bite. The man cleared his throat. "Given your youthful look, you must follow some kind of skin regimen."

"Nope."

"Then you must have excellent genetics, as you don't look your age at all."

"Blame a healthy diet of honey."

"Honey is not healthy. It's pure sugar."

"Exactly." She grinned as she turned, her thick knit sweater covering bountiful curves. She pulled on leggings in a bright plaid that hurt his eyes and didn't at all match the abominable snowman on the front of her shirt.

Rather than comment on her fashion sense, which took a lot of tongue biting, he went with, "Could I borrow a phone? I should contact the Pride so they're not worried."

"Already done, Simba. Who do you think told me to go looking for your frozen butt?"

"I can't believe they left without me." Felix thrived on being noticed. Yet since he'd arrived in America, only Arik's daughter had paid him any kind of attention. Had he lost his charming touch?

"In their defense, it was pure chaos what with the brewing storm, the two dozen trees, and the axe throwing."

He almost asked about the latter and then decided he really didn't want to know. "When should I expect transportation back to the city?"

"Two days, maybe three."

He stared at her as she pulled on thick woolen socks over the ankles and calves of her leggings.

"Pardon, but can you repeat that? I could have sworn you said two or three days."

"Could be sooner but also could be later. We got a hell of a storm overnight. Dumped a foot on the roads, and given I'm in the country, they won't be getting to mine anytime soon. Meaning most likely they won't plow my road before the next blizzard hits."

"Another storm is coming?" He ogled her, and not in a leering kind of way but more with the shock of the sky having more snow. "Didn't we already get a season's worth?"

She laughed, the belly kind that crinkled the corners of her eyes and lifted her lips. "It's expected to deposit another two to five inches at the minimum, but I'm thinking it will be closer to a foot."

"So I'm stuck here?"

"Yup." She popped the P as she moved past him for the stairs leading down from her loft bedroom. He spent a moment eyeing it, the massive king-sized bed, the dresser of clothes, some of the drawers half open, garments hanging over the edge, others balled and shoved in. More fabric littered the floor. The scent in this space one hundred percent her. No male. Or female for that matter.

He followed her to the main level. "Surely there must be a way I can get back to my cousin. It's sunny outside." He flung a hand in the direction of the window, blazing with light. "Won't that melt it?"

Edwina snorted. "This stuff ain't melting 'til spring. Best we can do is shovel the porch and driveway and hope the plow makes it down the road sooner rather than later."

A man of warm climates, he only half believed her. Surely it wasn't as bad as she claimed? He padded to a window radiating cold and looked out upon a winter land. A heavy blanket of snow had fallen and continued to lightly drift down despite the sunshine sparkling off all that glinting white grossness. And she said more was coming?

"Guess I'm stuck." Not part of his plan. Had he known, he'd have brought some essentials with him.

"That you are, Simba. Trust me, I'm not happy about it either. But it is what it is. Toast?" She offered him a thick slice she'd buttered.

"Is it processed or fresh?"

"It's food. So yes or no?"

"Yes." He'd detox and cleanse once he escaped. He took the thick slice and slathered it with the homemade jam she pulled from her fridge. She added honey to hers. It led to him staring as she took a bite, the glaze of sugar sticking to her lips, making him long for a taste.

"Not happening," she remarked suddenly.

"What isn't?"

"I know that look," she warned before taking another bite.

"What look?"

"The one that says you're horny and you'll fuck anything available, even me."

Only part of her statement was correct. He was horny, but he tended to be picky about who he had sex with. "What's that supposed to mean?"

"As if I need to explain. We both know I'm not your type."

"Oh really, and pray tell, what is my type?"

"I'm going to guess super thin, perfect makeup, and excellent ass-kissing skills."

"For your information, I prefer my women with curves." Big breasts being his weakness. And none of those silicone type that were too firm and didn't jiggle.

"If you say so."

"Why would I lie?"

"Because men like you will say anything to get what they want."

"Men like me? That sounds like an insult."

"More like a reality. You're a prince who is used to being fawned over by beautiful women. You've probably never had to work physically hard for anything in your life, and between your title, wealth, and looks, probably aren't used to going to bed alone."

"Why, Honeybear, did you just insult me?" He used the nickname on purpose.

She grinned. "Why yes I did. Good job on recognizing it. I was worried my peasant humor might not be up to your lofty ideals."

For some reason her unexpected reply made him laugh. "You're funny."

"Since when is the truth humorous?"

"When it's not entirely true. For your information, I do work, perhaps not lugging and cutting down trees, but in this day and age, I thought we'd gotten past measuring people's worth based on how much they can lift and carry."

"True, I shouldn't discount the effort needed waving to the peons when you trot by in your carriage drawn by white horses."

He gaped at her. "You don't seriously think that's how royalty travel?"

"No," she huffed, "but I kind of hoped. Please tell me you at least live in a real castle?"

The corner of his mouth quirked. "I do. But the plumbing is quite modern."

"I'm fine with that. I was worried you'd tell me you lived in some modern rowhouse or a condominium like your city cousins." She shuddered.

"You don't like living in proximity to people?"

"Would I live here by myself if I did?"

"It is rather quiet. And lonely." He didn't mean to say that part out loud, but she didn't take insult.

"Only lonely if you don't know how to keep busy. Between the trees, the honey, this house, my books, and four streaming services, I don't have time for anything else."

"Doesn't that get monotonous?"

"Not everyone likes to be go, go, go all the time. Some of us prefer a more laid-back approach to life."

That he could understand. After all, hadn't he eschewed the crown for that reason? He didn't want the stress, and yet, he couldn't imagine doing nothing with his life. He enjoyed his work as a perfumer and social media icon.

Which reminded him... He really should get online

and post some pics of his American adventure. "My coat? Where is it? I wonder if my phone is working." She pointed to a hook by the door.

The cell phone remained fried.

She noticed. "You can borrow mine if you'd like." She indicated it on the counter. With its two bars it would be good for a while yet, if he could get a signal.

"Is that a flip phone?"

"Yup."

"I thought those things went out of style a decade ago."

"Nope, you can still buy them."

"Why would you?"

"Because they're cheap and cool." She grabbed it, flipped it open, and whispered, "Beam me up, Scotty, 'cause there's no intelligent life down here."

"Ha. Ha."

She appeared completely unrepentant. "You're laughing, and yet guess whose phone is still working? And this despite falling in the toilet once, getting swarmed by bees—because apparently they can't stand a certain female music artist—and getting stolen by a squirrel."

The last part caught his attention and had him blurting out, "A squirrel attacked me in the woods."

"Sure, it did." She snorted.

"I swear. It pelted me with acorns and then made that tree fall on me. I think it might be a rabid killer."

She stared at him and then laughed. "Let me guess. It wore a red Santa hat."

"Aha! You know it. Does the evil rodent belong to you?"

"No, and the squirrel's name is Rudolph. Rudy for short. And he is a bit of a shit. Stole that hat you saw him wearing from the gnome my grandma left me." She gestured to a hairy goblin on the mantle, its eyes hidden behind the strands of gray, its nose a giant bulb.

"Why would he steal a hat?"

"Because he likes it? He's also taken my Christmas stocking, button collection, and a can of maple syrup."

"You should set a trap for the menace."

"If I laid snares for everything that annoyed me, I'd run out of places to bury the bodies." She gave him a pointed look.

Touché. "Since you're so attached, I will leave your little rodent alone."

"As if you could ever come close to catching Rudy." She took a last sip of her coffee and set the mug in the sink before sauntering past him for the door, where she layered up in a coat and boots.

"Where are you going?"

"Snow isn't going to shovel itself."

"I'll help."

She eyed his trendy ankle boots—that hurt his feet even looking at them. Edwina smirked. "You don't have the right equipment."

With that insult, she went outside and left him

simmering in annoyance alone. He couldn't have even said why exactly. If she wanted to shovel by herself, let her. He'd stay where it was nice and warm.

Like a spoiled prince. Just as she'd accused him of.

Sigh. He could very easily be the man she expected.

Or he could spend the time he was stuck here trying to figure out why the splendid Edwina preferred to live on a farm alone. And prove he wasn't a pampered brat.

He headed into the bedroom where he'd spent the night and rifled through the closets and drawers. He did his best not to cringe as he located gear to keep him warm. Some of it obviously old, none of it trendy, not even when new.

He emerged from her house to find the front porch partially cleared and a path in the snow leading to the oversized garage. As he neared, the galoshes on his feet threatening to fall off with each step—because her grandfather apparently had massive paws—he heard cursing.

"Goddamn piece of junk. Should have bought that new one when I was in town last week."

He entered the garage to find her leaning over a snowblower, yanking on its cord. It refused to start.

"Can I help?"

"As if you know how to fix a machine," she huffed, the last yank pulling the cord clean out. She went stumbling and landed hard on her ass.

Oof.

He stood over her and offered a hand. "I think it might be broken."

"No shit, Simba." She eyed him askance. "You're wearing Grandpa's clothes."

"You don't say. They seemed better suited for the climate."

"They look good on you." The words slipped out of her, and he could see her surprise.

Then again, she shouldn't be. "My sister claims I'd make a plastic bag look good."

"You and your sister are close?" Edwina asked.

"Does it count as close if she's told me I should model that plastic bag over my head?"

Edwina chuckled. "Proper siblings, then."

"If by proper you mean she's tried to kill me. Although not as much since I told her she could have the throne."

"You abdicated?"

"Of sorts. Technically, she is older than me, but historically the Pride is usually ruled by the oldest son. Unless he's not an alpha. Then there's a challenge. And things get ugly."

"Are women not allowed to challenge?" she asked as she stood, brushing off her ass.

"None ever did until my sister."

"And you didn't want to fight her."

"No kidding I didn't. She would have wiped the floor with me." Francesca could be very frightening.

Edwina gaped at him.

"What?"

"I can't believe you admitted that."

"No point in lying. I don't know anyone who's met my sister who wouldn't be afraid."

"Does it bother you that you won't be king?"

"Nope. Do you know how many babies you're expected to kiss? Sticky babies," he elucidated in case that wasn't clear.

"You don't like children?"

"Actually, I like them very much. I just don't want to be forced to smooch every single one thrust my way as if it's somehow good luck. I'd be fine with my own, as I know they'll be clean."

"Spoken by a man who has no idea," she muttered. She scowled at her broken machine. "I can't believe it died."

"Guess that means we're shoveling out by hand."

"Guess so," she sighed.

She grabbed a shovel by the door, and he grabbed the second before he followed her outside. He immediately regretted his offer. She really did have a lot of driveway.

"If you get too cold, just go inside," she advised as she began to scoop and dump the monstrous white stuff.

Tempting, but only an asshole would leave her alone to do it.

"How about we wager who finishes their side first?" he countered as he began to work alongside.

"What's the winner get?"

Given the amount of work to be done, only one prize appealed. "Full body massage?"

She grinned. "Oh, I am totally going to need one by the time we are done. You are on, Simba."

He tried to use his annoyance at her use of that stupid name to fuel his shoveling. It didn't last long.

Edwina beat him. Soundly. The woman shoveled like a machine, and when done, slapped him on the back, exclaiming, "I win. See you when you're done."

He eyed the twenty feet of driveway left to the road and almost cried. When he did finally finish, he wanted to crawl into a hot bubble bath and die. Not that he'd admit it.

He dragged his ass inside to find her bathed, dressed in a new godawful outfit that involved orange and fuchsia, feet propped in front of her fat-bellied wood stove, a steaming cup of cocoa in hand. Wet hair hung down her back, more of it than expected now that it was out of its tight braids.

She grinned at him. "I was starting to wonder if I'd have to go find you again."

"I can see why you use a snowblower. That was intense. Give me a second to thaw and I'll give you your prize." Knowing he'd lose and get to touch her was the only thing that kept him going.

"Go have a shower first. It'll help you thaw. There's

honey shampoo, conditioner, and body wash you can use."

"What brand?" he asked because he didn't use just anything in his hair.

"It's not something you can buy in a store. It's Grandpa's special recipe."

Scary. He could only hope it wouldn't cause any damage. The shower remained steamy, and he couldn't help but think of Edwina bathing before him. The water sluicing over those naked curves. Curves he'd get to massage.

He jerked off so quick at the thought he wondered if he had a problem. Especially since his dick twitched the moment he thought of Edwina.

Fascinating woman.

Schwing.

He eyed his dick, waving around in the shower, thinking it would get some action. He wouldn't count on it. Edwina had yet to act as expected. For one, she'd not yet crawled uninvited into his bed. Fallen on him claiming she tripped. Kissed him, calling him irresistible. However, she did seem keen on the massage.

Schwing.

Down, boy. Not yet.

He concentrated on the products available for cleansing. He didn't even have to pull off caps to smell the honey. The shampoo poured into his hand, a golden color that lathered nicely. The conditioner was a thick cream that left his hair feeling silky. The honey-scented body wash left his skin tingling in a good way.

Exiting the shower, a massive fluffy towel awaited, warm as it sat on a copper looping of pipe that he noticed ran to the shower. Clever. As he used the hot water, the pipe warmed, as did the towel hung over it. It worked better than some more expensive units he'd come across.

With the warm towel wrapped around his body, he stood in front of the mirror and eyed his wet hair. A smaller hand towel offered a brisk way of rubbing excess moisture. Many might have been surprised by how vigorously he scrubbed. Healthy hair had strong roots and a good manipulation of the scalp helped in that respect.

Once dried to his satisfaction, he located a brush, hers judging by the long dark strands caught in the bristles. Had it been a multipurpose brush he would have cleansed it, but the only scent was Edwina's. He ran the bristles through his hair, surprised by the lack of tangles. The true test would be when it dried and he got to see the color. Dull and matted or a perfect shiny gold without a hint of brassiness? He had a feeling it might be the latter. Edwina obviously sat on a treasure trove of recipes. It would explain why Mother told him to check out this farm. Her idea of being subtle.

Felix emerged to find Edwina in the kitchen, prepping a mug, which she handed to him. Cocoa topped with marshmallows. Simple and delicious.

He took a sip before saying, "I'm surprised there's no honey in it."

She uttered a chuckle. "It's one of the few things that doesn't need it."

"Speaking of honey. Those bathing products are quite nice. Have you ever thought of mass producing and selling them to the public?"

"Nope."

"Why not?"

"Because, while it is amazing, it is an arduous process just to create a supply for my family's personal use."

"Only because you're doing it by hand. We could automate the process."

"Still a no because the recipe is a family secret."

"What if I said you could make a fortune?" he cajoled.

"Not really an incentive. My family is already quite comfortable."

"Then how about just a peek at the recipe?" He offered a winsome smile.

It failed. "Nope."

"Why not?"

"Would you like a dictionary to look up the word 'secret'?"

"What if I wanted to buy some?"

"Sorry, not for sale to the public."

"But you do have stuff for sale. What do you have that I can buy?" Because her reluctance was like pulling on his tail—it wasn't just tigers that hated it.

"I'm afraid we only share that information with our active client list."

He'd have asked how to join, but he had a feeling she'd just shoot him down again. "Have you used the same honey products your entire life?"

"Why does it matter?"

He indicated her dried tresses. "Because you have great hair." A huge compliment coming from him.

"It's too long," she complained with a wrinkle of her nose. "I got it chopped six months ago. and it's grown a foot already."

Surely she exaggerated.

"Does your entire family have hair as thick as yours?" he asked. "Any balding?"

"Nah, although Grandpa and Dad have gone gray. Mom's hair is as dark as mine still."

"And do you think that's because of your honey products?"

She rolled her eyes. "What is this obsession with my hair? Next thing you'll be asking to grope it."

"Can I touch?"

Her lips quirked. "I assume we're still talking about my hair."

"Yes, although I wouldn't be averse to touching you elsewhere." It slipped out before he could stop it.

Many women would have batted their lashes and offered a come-hither response. Not Edwina.

She snorted. "I'm not that desperate."

"What's that supposed to mean?" he asked as she whirled to give him access to her long tresses, still damp in places, yet their silken nature shone through.

"You're not my type. I like my men big and burly, not afraid to get dirty."

"I can get dirty," he rumbled.

She cast him a glance and a quirked lip as she said, "I'm not talking about the bedroom kind."

"You keep implying I'm useless, and I'd like to know why you've jumped to that assumption."

She grabbed his left hand and pointed to the palm. "No calluses."

"And?"

"Real working people have them."

"Only because they don't care for themselves. I'm a believer in caring for my body. We only get the one, you know." He flipped her hands over and traced the pads of her fingers. "Yours aren't very rough."

"Because of the honey balm I use to prevent chapping."

"Meaning someone might mistake you for being soft."

Her laughter erupted. "That's never happened."

"Well, I promise you, these hands are strong, even if they're not rough on the skin. I'll prove it."

"How?"

"I owe you a massage."

"Bah. Forget it. You're probably sore after all that shoveling."

"A bet is a bet," he insisted. "Sit."

He pushed her onto a stool and stood behind her, losing himself for a moment in the scent of her. Honey and woman and cuddly bear. He hesitated to put his hands on her, mostly because he really wanted to touch her. Desired her and, despite what she might claim, it wasn't desperation. Felix had never been the type to be overcome by passion. But then again, he'd never met anyone like Edwina.

"Is this one of those new age massages that doesn't involve touching?" She grumbled a complaint as he hesitated too long.

"I thought bears were the patient sort."

"Because you've obviously met so many." He didn't need to see her face to know she rolled her eyes.

"In my position, I've actually encountered more than a few."

"Oh, and what have you learned about my kind?"

"That for one, bears vary depending on where they're raised. For example, never try to out-drink a Russian bear. The French are very particular about cheese. And if you think pandas are cuddly and sweet, that's only true so long as you don't screw up their tea ceremony."

"What about American bears?"

"I'm still figuring you out." His hands kneaded her shoulders, digging in and finding the hard knots in her muscles, working them, and drawing a sigh from her as her body loosened.

He worked his way down her spine and resisted an urge to continue the massage on her front. Instead, he knelt and handled her feet, almost getting kicked in the face as she giggled, a sweet, unexpected sound.

He glanced up to see her sheepishly grinning. "Sorry. Ticklish."

"I'll be careful, then." He massaged her feet until she groaned instead of chuckled and worked his way up her calves, digging into those muscles. She truly had a toned body, that of a hard-working woman.

With a sweet scent.

He could smell her arousal. Not a thing she could hide. But not something he could act upon without her permission. Still, he had to remove himself from temptation.

He stood between her legs, and she eyed him, eyes at half mast, lips parted. Soft. Sensual. "Done already?"

"Depends. Are you still feeling tense?" He placed a hand on her thigh and felt the subtle quiver in her flesh.

"You might say I'm a little tight still."

"Oh. Did you need me to work you some more?" He slid his hand until he cradled the crevice between her leg and groin. Close enough he could feel the pulse of her burgeoning arousal.

"Are you sure you're up to it?" A gentle tease.

He leaned in, lips hovering a hairsbreadth from hers. "I'm—"

Power suddenly returned and, with it, bright lights and noise that ruined the mood.

Edwina suddenly shifted away from him and said, "Power is a good sign, as it means they're clearing the roads and the crews are able to get around. Shouldn't be long now before you're rescued."

She headed for the living room, and he stared, praying like he'd never prayed before for another storm to keep him here.

CHAPTER SEVEN

ON THE EVE OF THE FIFTH DAY OF BEARMAS, A PRINCE GAVE TO ME – A REASON TO DIG OUT SOME BATTERIES.

The power didn't remain on for long, as a second storm rolled in. Good thing Edwina had a propane-fueled stove for cooking and hot water. As for her dead fridge, she'd already placed everything outside in a cooler to keep it from spoiling. If needed, she could always fire up the generator for some power.

She'd have sworn Felix looked pleased as he stared out the window at the darkening sky, somber with new falling snow. "Guess I'll be stuck here a while longer." An almost gleeful statement.

He might be happy, but Edwina teetered more on the edge of frustration. Blame him for managing to arouse her. Surprising given she wasn't even sure she liked the vain cat. But she would give him credit. He'd jumped in to help without complaint and then honored the bet he'd lost. If the electricity hadn't ruined the moment, who knew what might have happened.

Okay, she did know. They would have done the horizontal bear tango. However, it was one thing to sleep with a prince she barely knew in the almost dark; another to do it eyes wide open.

Although, in retrospect, she couldn't have said what made it different. It wasn't as if it would mean anything. Sex with no strings. She did it all the time and would wager he did, too. Yet, for some reason, it felt different with Felix. The way her skin prickled when he got near, her awareness of him, and what about his scent did she find so delicious? Ever since she'd brought his ice-cubed butt back and he'd thawed out, she'd noticed it. It made her mouth water, something usually only reserved for Grandpa's honied salmon and Mom's honey cakes.

Her very attraction only served to make her leery. Hence why she spent the few hours they had of electricity getting a load of laundry done—because apparently, she'd need clean underpants if he stayed—and downloading some movies to her laptop, which she also charged, along with her phone.

Which had more than a few messages. All from the Pride lions.

Arik started with an apology. *Sorry you've been inconvenienced. You'll be compensated.*

She replied, *No worries.*

A normal conversation to have.

It was the biatches who took it one step too far.

Did you and the prince have to snuggle to keep warm last night? Asked by a no-boundaries Melly.

So, do you need to be rescued, or do you want to ride that lion into the ground before sending him back wrung out and dry? A bold query by Luna.

Meena just sent emojis. Peach. Eggplant. Fireworks and a heart.

As for Joan, she sent a crying face lion, a special icon only the Pride appeared to have access to.

Why did everyone assume she and the prince hooked up?

Sure, he actually seemed quite nice and not so snobbish when it was just the two of them. He'd pitched in and helped her around the cabin, sorting things out, getting ready for the next power failure.

He'd relayed witty stories and actually showed a sharp wit. Not to mention a good sense of humor that didn't get offended when she teased him about his hair and skin regime.

In her defense, seeing a man run the muscles of his face through a strange undulating exercise to keep them loose and prevent wrinkles begged for some ridicule. However, she would admit that watching him do some yoga to stretch his muscles was something to drool over.

She thought of him, bent over, ass in the air when she went to bed that night.

Alone.

Despite watching a movie, their chairs glued side by side to share the laptop screen, he acted the perfect gentleman, unaffected by her presence at all.

She couldn't say the same. It took her a while to fall asleep, and when she woke abruptly, she didn't wonder why for long.

"What do you want?" she grumbled, finding the prince standing once more in her room, wearing Grandpa's plaid pajama bottoms and with an almost matching shirt. It shouldn't have been sexy. What did it say that she wished he'd just slipped into the warm bed with her? The man appeared sturdier than first thought. Enough to handle a strenuous ride?

"I heard something," he said rather than taking off his pants, meaning she really was awake and this wouldn't turn into a sticky dream.

"It's an old house. It creaks." She rolled over in her bed and, as she did, noticed her vibrator on the nightstand, barely visible in the light filtering through the window from the three-quarter moon. But still, what if he saw?

She quickly whipped her hand out and drew it under the covers so he wouldn't notice.

He noticed given his drawled, "Are you what I heard?"

"What did you hear?"

"Something definitely motorized."

Wait, was he telling her he heard her masturbating earlier? Some women might have hidden at being discovered self-pleasuring. Edwina didn't care. "I'm surprised you could hear it given the batteries were practically dead," she drawled as she rolled over to own her sexuality. She met his amused gaze.

"Unless you hooked it up to a generator in the last few minutes, then I don't think the noise came from you. Sounded like an engine."

"Probably the snowplow going by."

"Except it came from the woods."

That got her attention. She sat up, and the sheet fell to her waist, baring her breasts. His gaze slipped to them. A second ago, she'd have arched her back in subtle invitation, but now she had questions.

"What makes you think it came from the woods? Did you see anything?"

He shook his head. "I haven't gone out to look yet. Thought I should let you know first."

She rolled out of bed, not wearing any pajamas. His gaze lingered on her breasts. Her nipples tightened —and not because the chilly air kissed them.

"Is it still snowing?" she asked, moving for the pile of clothes she'd tossed onto a chair.

"No, but the wind is whipping it around, making visibility shit at random moments."

"And you're sure you heard something?" Totally possible he had since she practically hibernated once she went to sleep.

"Yeah, but at the same time, how? I mean, the roads

are snow jammed, and it's not like you can drive through your forest."

"Not on four wheels, but a snowmobile wouldn't have any problems." Although why anyone would be out this time of night and on her farm of all places was a whole other question. "Stay here while I check it out."

"I don't think so."

"It'll be cold and dark, Simba."

"I'll layer up to stay warm."

"You'll mess up your precious hair."

"Then I'll comb it when we both return."

He countered all her arguments. "Whatever. I'll get dressed and be down in a second." Not that she really wanted to go outside at the un-bearly hour of 2 a.m., but a farmer didn't always keep regular hours. Even one who tended bees and trees.

Only as she tugged on a sweater Grandma had knitted with a psychedelic arrangement of snowflakes did it occur to her that it might be better if she went poking around as a bear. While unlikely she deal with intruders—because only idiots would be out in this storm—she'd move more quickly and have enhanced senses as her ursine.

She went down the steps to find the prince fully dressed and waiting, barely visible in the gloom. His teeth flashed as he said, "Might want some pants. It's chilly outside."

"I'm gonna poke around as my bear. See if I catch any scents."

"Any reason why someone would be coming around at night?"

"Not any good ones." It had been a long time since they'd had to deal with tree thieves. Grandpa and Mom had taught the would-be ax murderers a lesson they never forgot.

"Do you have a weapon I can use?"

"We are a gun-free home. But there is a baseball bat in the umbrella stand."

"What about one of those axes you had the other day?"

"In the shed, which I can already tell you is probably partially buried in a snowdrift. So unless you want to spend some time digging, I'd go with the bat."

Not to mention, she wasn't about to arm him with a sharp blade. What if he had bad aim and lopped off a crucial part?

"Should we call the police?"

"And say what? You heard a noise?"

His lips clamped tight. "Forgive me. In my home, noises in the middle of the night are treated with extreme care."

"Listen, double oh kitty, this is a honey and Christmas tree farm, not some kind of secret base of operations, munitions hideaway, or anything else that would make this place a target of anything super nefarious."

"Yet you're getting dressed and readying to go out in that storm."

"Because if someone did just come through the woods on a snowmobile or something, then I want to know why. Maybe they're in trouble."

"Or they're after someone."

She snorted. "You? Why would anyone come after you? I thought your sister was queen."

"Queen in waiting. My mother is still alive."

"I thought your sister was the first woman to take on the role."

"First one to inherit. It has happened a few times that strong alpha queens have taken over the Pride when their husbands died and the heirs required maturing."

"And what does that have to do with someone wanting to kill you?"

"Nothing. Other than to say I have been targeted in the past."

"And obviously escaped given you're sitting here."

"We're sitting prey."

"Hardly. Don't worry, Prince Simba. I'll protect you." She patted him on the arm before she stripped her shirt, tossed it onto a kitchen chair, and headed outside, hoping he had the brains to shut the door behind her.

The moment she hit the porch, she smelled it, burning oil and exhaust. The prince hadn't imagined the motor noise. Someone had recently passed by on a snowmobile. She followed the lingering scent trail to her barn, a massive structure, weather tight, lacking windows, and while it did have giant doors on both sides, she found the motorized sled parked by the much smaller, access door. She sniffed the sled, not one she recognized. A beaten-up Arctic Cat covered in peeling and faded stickers. No driver, the keys left in the ignition. The overwhelming stench of burning hid all other scents.

She nosed around her building despite knowing the driver of the sled had gone in through the side door. Best make sure they didn't have an accomplice before she followed them inside. The snow around the perimeter remained undisturbed, so once she completed the circuit, she was ready to confront whoever had broken into her barn, a barn that sheltered her precious beehives during the winter months.

To her surprise, the prince appeared to have already entered while she scouted the far side. She smelled him by the door, which he'd shut, meaning she had to shift to open it. Chilly on her naked bits. She quickly entered the barn, which was much less frigid than outside, but dark given the power remained out. The only reason the vast space retained a bit of heat was because of the solar panels giving juice to heaters that kept the space from going into a deep freeze.

Rather than uselessly click the light switch, she ran her fingers along the top lintel of the door where she kept a lighter stashed for the lantern she kept on a hook just above the same door. Grandpa always said redundant systems, like extra light in a little used barn, only seemed dumb until you needed them. It took a few clicks before the wick ignited and she could see somewhat.

The nimbus of light showed a line of hives, three rows of them, going eight deep. The rows stood almost as tall as her, deceptive sentinels that blocked her view. They didn't, however, hide the huffs of exertion as the prince tussled with someone.

They'd better not knock over any of her bees' homes. Each one held a precious queen. Once winter loosened its grip on the land, the boxes would be moved to the apiaries, fields specifically set aside for the bees. If they survived.

She winced as one of her hives tottered, the sound of it a distinctive rattle. But it gave her a direction to head. Lantern held aloft, she went past the first row of hives. Between the fifth and sixth she found the combatants.

Felix wrestled with another man, dressed head to toe in winter gear, including a baclava and goggles. As she watched, the not-so-feeble prince jabbed the intruder once, twice in the face. He'd obviously taken some boxing lessons. The intruder swung and didn't even come close to striking. Felix's next blow connected. There was a yelp as a nose crunched. The smell of blood filled with the air, as did blubbering.

"Mutha-fucka." A wet gurgled complaint.

Felix hauled the person to their feet and shook them, growling, "Who are you? What are you doing here?"

While Edwina didn't know what he was doing at the farm, she did recognize the intruder. This close, despite the baclava and goggles, no mistaking the scent. "This is Barry Kolman. My ex-boyfriend."

CHAPTER EIGHT

ON THE FIFTH DAY OF CHRISTMAS, A GREEN-EYED MONSTER GAVE TO ME — A SERIOUS CASE OF JEALOUSY.

For some reason, hearing the word boyfriend had Felix wanting to hit the guy he'd tackled inside Edwina's barn. Smack him again and again.

Him, jealous? Never.

The only thing he ever envied was excellent hair on other people. But knowing this man used to touch Edwina—

Whack.

"Ow. What the fuck?" The wimp—a human by scent—reeled, holding his face.

"Yeah, what the fuck, Barry?" Edwina snapped angrily at her ex. Would she mind if he hit Barry again?

"He hit me," Barry accused, whining.

It curled Felix's lip. "Want me to hit you again?" Felix really hoped he'd say yes.

"Hold off there, Rocky." She held up a hand in Felix's direction and turned her ire on Barry, a man a few inches taller than Felix and probably a foot wider. Was this the type of male that attracted her? "What are you doing here?" Edwina asked.

"A better question is, why are you naked?" Barry pushed up his goggles and ogled her curves.

Felix rumbled in discontent. "Eyes averted or I will remove them."

His threat caused Edwina to laugh. "Let him look. If he touches, though, you can eat him."

Oh hell yeah he would. Despite hoping the guy tried something, Felix decided to not tempt the fucker and shrugged off his borrowed coat to drape around Edwina.

"Who the fuck is this guy?" Barry jerked his thumb at Felix.

"None of your business."

"I'm making it my business." Barry seemed to think he could intimidate Edwina. It didn't work of course. Probably explained why he was an ex-boyfriend.

"Enough." Edwina snapped her fingers. "No changing the subject. Why are you here?"

Barry pulled his broken goggles off the rest of the way and tossed them before he peeled off his blood-soaked face covering, which didn't improve his appearance. "I knew the power was out in your area and the roads blocked, so I came to check on you."

Skepticism arched her brow. "At three in the morning?"

"I couldn't sleep?" He didn't sound certain of his own lie.

"And chose to check on me by breaking into my barn?"

"I didn't want to wake you, so I was going to stay warm in here until you woke."

"Bullshit," Felix exclaimed.

"I wasn't talking to you, asshole. Who the fuck are you anyhow?" Barry glowered in his direction.

Before Felix could reply, Edwina tugged him into a half-hug. "This is my boyfriend, Simba."

"You're dating? Since when?" Barry exclaimed.

"Since I found a pretty man who knows his way around a woman's body. Unlike some people I used to know."

Felix almost grinned at the dig even as he knew she lied to annoy her ex.

"I don't believe it. I've never seen this guy around before."

She arched a brow. "Spying on me, Barry?"

Realizing he'd fucked up, Barry changed tactics. "I care about you, Winnie."

She winced. "Don't call me that. You know I hate that name."

"What can I say? You're just so cute and cuddly like the bear." Barry tried to be charming, and Edwina scowled even harder.

"And that's just one of the reasons we're not a couple," she muttered.

"I would have thought it was because all the steroids he took made him dumb," Felix offered, hoping Barry would take the bait and attack him first so he could hit him hard.

"Fuck off." Barry snapped verbally instead of with his fist. "I'm trying to talk to Edwina."

"Well, I don't want to chat with you. It's like four in the morning."

"I couldn't wait a second longer to admit my feelings for you."

"What feelings? Because I do believe when I broke things off you said I was a fat-assed, boring sow and you could do better."

"I was upset at the time. I didn't mean it."

"And it took you this long to come apologize?"

"I figured you were angry and needed time to cool off."

"Why would I be angry? Your opinion literally means nothing."

"I see you're still mad."

"No, more annoyed I have to deal with you. We didn't even date that long. What was it, like a month?"

"Almost three months. The best of my life."

Edwina's laughter barked louder than Felix's astonishment. "I can't believe you just said that. What a load of poop. Now enough with the shit. What's the real reason you broke into my barn?"

"I didn't break in." A strange rebuttal to make given where they argued.

It was Felix who said, "He's got two sets of keys on him." He could smell the metal.

"My missing keys. You took them!" She glanced at Felix to add, "Thought I lost them." To Barry, she said, "You took them that night you stayed over."

"We were dating. It was my right."

"Like hell it was," she growled. "You should have given them back when I told you I wouldn't be seeing you anymore."

"I assumed it would be temporary."

"Are you deluded? Do you really think I'd take you back after the way you freaked out? I can only imagine what you would have done if we'd been alone instead of in public."

Wait, was Edwina worried this guy might hurt her?

"I never laid a hand on you."

"Because you didn't have a chance. And before you falsely claim you'd never, I'm aware of your arrest record for assault. At least you're progressive enough you hit both men and women."

Felix ogled Barry. "At your size? What kind of asshole are you?"

"The kind who needs to leave. Right after he hands over my keys." Edwina held out her hand.

"Ask me nicely." Barry really didn't get it.

Felix slugged him in the gut and said, "Keep them. I can do this all day."

Alas, Barry pussied out. A jangling set of keys emerged.

Edwina snatched them. "You better not have made copies."

"Or what? Gonna sic your boyfriend on me?"

"No need when I can hit you myself," she snarled.

"You wouldn't hurt me."

"Do you really want to test me on that?"

"Don't you dare threaten me. I know people." Barry had the nerve to admonish.

"Did none of those people tell you it was an idiotic idea to ride around in the dark in a snowstorm?"

"I came out here with heroic intentions." The man puffed out his chest as he lied. Thick. Muscled. But Felix already knew it was pretty rather than useful.

"I don't need rescuing. As you can see, I'm fine."

"Don't look fine given you're out in the cold with no clothes. Did this man chase you from your home in the storm?"

Felix arched a brow, but once more, before he could even formulate a reply, Edwina had one. A good one.

"Oh, he was chasing me all right. As part of our foreplay." Once more she hugged him tight to her side, and it was all he could do not to take advantage. "It's called polar plunge sex. Very good for getting the blood flowing. Although, someone like you, lacking in the endowment department, might want to be careful so you don't freeze off the little bit you've got."

It took all of Felix's strength to not burst out laughing at the expression on Barry's face.

"Why you fucking c—"

Barry didn't finish the sentence. Felix's fist did.

The prone man groaned as Edwina stood over him and offered an amused, "Did I forget to mention Simba takes my honor seriously?"

Barry hadn't learned his lesson apparently. "Your boyfriend is welcome to your fat ass."

When Felix hauled him to his feet for another punch, Edwina put a hand on his chest. "It's okay, my brave lion. We both know Barry is just sour because he wasn't man enough to handle me and you are."

Felix thrust the other man from him so he could drag Edwina close. His hands cupped those luscious cheeks, and he couldn't help but growl, "You are perfect, Honeybear."

For a moment she stared at him, her breath partially caught between parted lips. Her eyes wide. She probably thought he was playing up the moment for Barry.

He meant every damned word. And to prove it, he kissed her. Would have kissed her forever if someone didn't gag. A growl of annoyance rumbled from them both as they turned to the intruder wiping his bloody nose while leaning on a hive.

"Fucking gag me," a nasally Barry whined.

"Get out," she ordered.

"I will, but I'll be filing a complaint with the cops for assault," Barry stated.

"Go right ahead. And then I'll file mine. Trespassing, breaking and entering, assault on my boyfriend." She ticked off her fingers.

"He hit me first!" Barry pointed out.

"In self-defense," she countered. "What did you expect, lurking around like a burglar? You're lucky my grandpa isn't here, or you'd be fertilizing next year's wildflowers for the bees."

Barry gaped. "What the fuck? Are you threatening to kill me?"

"Me?" She blinked her lashes innocently. "I would never."

"But I would," Felix offered with a predatory smile.

A slack-jawed Barry finally had nothing to retort.

"You say the hottest things," Edwina drawled, bussing Felix's cheek.

"I would rather be doing things instead." Felix offered an evil eye to Barry, who swallowed hard.

"Sounds promising. Let me get rid of the trash." She pointed to Barry. "Out. Now." She probably should have grilled him more on his motives for coming, but it was the middle of the night and she had company.

Barry opened his mouth, and Felix smiled as he said, "Go ahead and say something stupid. I have no problem finding a shovel to bury your body."

"I know just the spot," Edwina quipped.

Barry finally got the hint and stomped off. A moment later they heard the whir of the snowmobile. This time with its light on, given Barry left behind the broken night vision goggles he'd been wearing before. A man who came prepared.

Felix crouched to snare them and dangled them by the strap. "He was lying about his reason for coming."

"You don't say."

"We should have questioned him more on his real reason for breaking in."

"Probably after one of my prized queens."

"I might be from overseas, but even I'm not so gullible as to believe there is a market for honeybees."

"Not just any bees. My queens. Do you know how many offers my family has fended over the years?"

"An offer to buy is a far cry from someone heisting. Is that why you think your ex was here? Could he have found out they're valuable?"

"You didn't believe he suddenly couldn't stand to live without my effervescent personality?"

"I think I can't believe you dated him for three minutes, let alone months."

She wrinkled her nose. "I was bored. He was available and sturdy. I honestly thought things were over. I'm not the type men pine over."

The claim bothered. "Why would you say that?"

"You heard what he said." She shrugged. "And don't think I say that for pity or motivational speeches about how great I am. I know I am great, and maybe one day I'll meet someone who agrees. Until then, I will use the Barrys of this world to scratch an itch."

Felix bit his tongue before he couldn't take back

the words hovering on his tongue—*I think you're great*. Instead, he chose to say, "How come you don't have an alarm system?"

She snorted. "It's honey, not maple syrup. No need for such strict measures. Not that it would have mattered. Power is out."

"You should maybe look into upgrading given you're out here by yourself. It's a good thing I was around."

Edwina scoffed. "Please. As if I needed help against a human."

"Never underestimate them. Not to mention a lover scorned can be the most dangerous thing after a wounded beast."

"I could have handled it."

"You shouldn't have to. There's no excuse for a man who doesn't listen when a woman says no."

She patted his cheek. "You're almost cute when you're being unnecessarily protective."

Almost cute?

He gaped as she slipped off his coat and handed it back. "You'll need this if you're going to keep your precious flesh from getting frostbite."

"What about you?"

"What about me?" she quipped and winked. "In case you hadn't noticed, this bear has back." She waggled it at him as she sauntered away, the teasing almost enough to have him reach for her and show her just how much he liked that ass.

Before he could do anything, she flipped back into her bear shape. She eyed him then the door, the hint being obvious. He held it open and watched as she lumbered back out into the storm.

Ugh. He really would prefer to stay inside where the snow didn't whip his face. But he wasn't about to leave her alone. What if Barry hadn't truly left, or he'd not come alone? There was more to the man's break-in than his supposed obsession with Edwina. Felix glanced around the barn with its covered hives hiding the wintering bees.

Surely the human hadn't been trying to steal them? There was no way he could have transported even one on that snowmobile of his. So what was his true goal? Hopefully not to hurt Edwina, who had gone off alone.

Felix exited into the frigid air and thought longingly of the warm bed he'd left. Soon he'd be back under the covers. He hoped.

Using the keys they'd retrieved from Barry, he locked the barn before he followed the bear tracks that went in the same direction as the trail left by the snowmobile. She appeared to be making sure Barry actually left.

Hard to believe she'd dated the guy. Sure, he was pretty with passable hair but obviously an ass. And a human. A surprising choice, although not unheard of. Shifters did need to keep their blood lines from getting stale, meaning they did marry outside their Prides or, in this case, Sleuths. Bears, having low birth rates compared to lions, had even less choice when it came to mating with their own kind.

Was Edwina the type to want to get married?

Felix had no interest, although he had felt a spurt of pleasure when she'd called him her boyfriend. Weird because he usually avoided involvement of any kind despite what the gossip rags claimed. The tabloids were always too quick to assume that any woman he smiled at was his bride-to-be. Apparently, a single prince wasn't to be borne.

He'd barely trailed her into the woods when she emerged, her dark fur frosted at the tips by the icy weather. She brushed against him as she lumbered past, and he followed that wiggle back into the house.

As he peeled off his outer layers, she shifted back to skin once more and headed for her potbellied stove.

Such a nice ass. What would she do if he stripped and joined her? Would she cuff him and tell him to put on some pants or encourage him to slip into her from behind, finger her in the front, and bite her neck as he thrust her to orgasm?

In the midst of this erotic thought, she turned around and said, "You coming?"

CHAPTER NINE

ON THE FIFTH DAY OF BEARMAS, A LION GAVE ME TO ME — THE FEMALE VERSION OF BLUE BALLS. SOMEONE HAND ME A JAR OF HONEY "O."

Felix appeared almost cross-eyed and didn't move. Poor delicate prince. Probably frozen. So she gestured again. "Come. Warm yourself."

He took a hesitant step then another, snaring the sweater hung over her chair in passing, which he handed to her. Odd he wanted her to cover up given she'd noticed his smoldering gaze and the erection he couldn't hide in those loose sleep pants.

The man wanted her, and he better watch himself or he'd find himself bearmauled since she felt the same way. Something about Felix, despite their major differences, appealed. Obviously a sign she needed to start dating again. But a better caliber than the Barrys of this world.

In her defense, she'd hoped by dating a human she'd not run into the misogyny often present in the shifter world. Bears being especially bad—her dad and

Grandpa being the exception mostly because Grandma would have skinned them herself.

However, the same couldn't be said about other male ursines. Every single time she'd gone to a bear picnic—which actually was a thing involving many hibachis and coolers on wheels—she'd been subjected to round-bellied men who thought she should fetch them snacks and drinks or scratch their backs. Needless to say, those men died of starvation and thirst, plagued by an itch.

In other words, she'd have died first before she served them.

Barry hadn't made demands of her, although he did forget his wallet often when they went out. Still, he served a means to an end, that end being an orgasm with another person. Despite his sturdy size, she'd had to be gentle lest she break him. It put a damper on her ardor at the time. Passion shouldn't require limits.

Could Felix handle her if she let loose in the bedroom? The man originally came off as a pampered buffoon' however, having seen him in action in the barn, she had to wonder how much of that might be an act. Her prince might have more depth than she'd given him credit for. If so, why pretend?

He did his best to ignore her as he warmed his hands over the stove.

As if. It wasn't just lionesses who could be forthright. "What do you do for a living other than kiss babies and shake hands?"

He snorted. "As if I'd subject myself to those kinds of microbes."

"I'm sure you carry around antibacterial spray for those occasions."

The corners of his lips lifted. "Can't be too careful. And in reply, I work for the family company. Charlemagne, Inc. We dabble in a few things but are most well-known for our perfumes."

"What's your job? Salesman?"

"Custom perfume designer."

That made her laugh. "Seriously?"

"Very. And before you mock, I will add that it's not a simple task creating fragrances that will mesh with people's scents. Everyone is unique and a well-balanced perfume requires careful chemical composition to achieve the proper result."

She angled her head. "I actually don't disagree. Honey is similar in that the pollen of different plants will achieve various attributes and flavors that are further augmented by the length of curing."

"I guess you would understand." He offered her a smile. "So, are you going to ask me?"

Ask him what? If he'd like to romp? Why should she be the one to make that first move? "Ask you what?" she replied.

"What scent would become you?"

"That's easy. Honey."

His laughter tickled her inside. "Yes, definitely a

part of it. But I'd also add a hint of cedarwood to counter the sweetness with your strength. And rose."

"Why?"

"Because it's sexy, like you."

"Oh." He'd left her speechless again. She changed the subject. "How often do you visit your cousin Arik?"

"Not often, I'm afraid. Although, if our planned partnership works out, I might be spending more time here. We're thinking of branching out our operations and establishing a base in America."

"Who will be running it?"

"That's a good question." He glanced at her, his gaze lingering on the way the sweater ended high on her thigh. "I'm thinking maybe I need a change of scenery."

"Only if you invest in better boots." She wrinkled her nose, and he laughed despite the dig.

"Boots. Coat. Gloves." He shook his head. "I will admit to being woefully underprepared. In my defense, I've never been anywhere this cold or snowy."

"You can't tell me you're a royal who's never gone skiing."

"I was more into yachts and beaches. What about you? Have you travelled?"

"Depends on if Florida counts. Given our business is seasonal, pretty much the only free time I have is after Christmas until the spring melt."

"Wait, you've never left the USA?"

She shook her head.

"You have to visit Europe."

"I'll admit it's an intriguing place but not the kind of trip you do alone if you really want to see and taste all there is to offer."

"I could show you around." His eyes widened as he made the offer, and her lips quirked.

"A prince stooping to being a tour guide? What would the tabloids say?"

His eyes twinkled as he said with a grin, "They would say you're my secret baby mama and have us engaged and married within twenty-four hours."

"That's horrifying," she exclaimed.

He stared at her long enough she shifted her weight before he replied, "I think that would depend on who they think I should be with."

"They obviously want to see you with a princess."

"Don't be so sure. My country is very romantic. They would also enjoy the story of their prince going to a foreign land and becoming beguiled by a local farmer."

The conversation shifted into territory she wasn't ready for. "I'm hungry. Are you hungry?" She desperately tried to ignore what he implied.

"Starving." His gaze went to her breasts, hidden by the bulky sweater.

"How about some honey-glazed cinnamon rolls?"

"You have some hidden? Where?"

"I don't have a stash if that's what you're thinking. I have to make them, Simba."

"You bake?"

"I didn't get these hips from eating salads." She laughed, and she might have put a bit more wiggle than necessary into her walk as she headed for her kitchen. She also bent over rather than crouch as she gathered the things she needed.

Despite what she thought was clear invitation, Felix joined her without a single slap to the butt. He sat at a stool on the other side of the butcher block island. Why did he have to be so hard to read? One minute he seemed into her, and the next he ignored a perfectly good opportunity to either smack her bottom or say something dirty about it.

Instead, he was a royal gentleman and made small talk. "Someone mentioned your family is in Florida?"

"Yeah, they leave after the bees are secured for winter. My parents were the first to go a few years ago now, claiming they'd prefer to hibernate somewhere warm. Not that they actually sleep as much anymore since they got there. Grandpa hemmed and hawed but finally joined them for the first time."

"So this is your first Christmas alone?"

"Not exactly. While I now live alone, I'll be joining them in Florida on Christmas Eve. Flight is already booked. Just waiting for the last-minute tree buyers before I go."

"You're leaving in a few days, then." His lips turned down for a moment before he caught himself.

"Yup. What about you? How long are you staying for?"

"I don't know. Guess that depends."

"On?"

"If I have a reason to stay." Once more his gaze settled on her, and she didn't have a reply.

Unless the moisture between her legs counted. Damn it. Would the smell of her rising dough cover it? "I need to let the rolls rise before I bake them. While they're doing that, I'm going to shower."

He remained seated while she headed for the bathroom. He didn't ask to join her, didn't knock or peek through the door she left unlocked.

Stupid of her to think he might be tempted. More likely it was only their forced proximity making him horny. It certainly was doing a number on her. She took a hot shower, followed by a blast of cold. It was only as she toweled herself off that she realized she hadn't brought her robe back down from the last time. Not usually a big deal. Nudity among shifters was normal. And this was her house. Explain why then she felt self-conscious as she emerged wrapped in a towel.

Felix had moved to the chair in the living room area and was reading a book. He held it up as she appeared.

"I never realized how interesting bees could be."

"They are fascinating not only because of the honey but their social structure." Despite only wearing a damp length of fabric, she launched into a spiel about queens and their drones. He didn't mock her or fall asleep but rather engaged with her and related his own stories about flowers, even suggesting a few that might provide interesting pollens.

"I can have some samples and seeds sent to you," he offered.

"I'd like that." She sat in the chair across from him, towel still tucked, but no longer self-conscious.

"Or instead of me sending seeds, you could come and visit, see the flowers in person."

"Um." The offer stunned her to silence. The timer in the kitchen went off. "I should get those buns in the oven."

As she rose from the chair, her towel snagged and unraveled. She didn't grab it in time and then didn't want to, as he fairly smoldered as he stared. She'd never been as aware of her nudity or herself as a woman more than in that moment. Desire unfurled, wanting and demanding. A desire reciprocated as he stood and drew near.

"I really should bake those buns," she murmured.

"There's only one thing I'd like to eat right now," he murmured huskily.

A corny thing to say, which meant there was only one thing to do. Mash her mouth against his.

Their lips hit in a hard clash. A rough passion unleashed that led to them pushing and shoving for dominance. He won.

She ended up with the island pressed into her

lower back, her head angled back as he kissed his way down the side of her neck. He spent only a little bit of time nibbling that flesh as he worked his way down to her breasts. He cupped them, a heavy handful in each palm, his thumbs stroking over the tips. He pushed them together and buried his face between them, rubbing the grizzled edge of his jaw against the tender skin.

She shuddered.

But she squirmed when he blew hotly against her nipples. She shook, and moisture pooled between her legs as he hovered his mouth just in front of a hopeful tip, teasing her. She went almost cross-eyed with her need.

"Tell me what you want."

She wanted him to seduce her. To manhandle her. To take her so hard, she came without needing extra aid.

But she couldn't say that aloud.

So instead, she relied on the ladle in the honey jar and drizzled some on her breasts.

He dove in for the feast. As his hands massaged her heavy breasts, kneading them, his lips pinched each of her nipples, one at a time, sucking and tugging the liquid honey from her flesh.

She groaned.

But he wasn't done. His breath fanned over the moist skin. He took his time, pinching a nipple with his lips, sometimes grazing with his teeth. The one not being sucked on he rolled between his fingers. She felt it as if he played between her legs, jolting pleasurable shocks that had her writhing and whimpering at his touch. He buried his face between her breasts, rubbing his roughened jaw against the soft skin, teasing it with some hard sucks that left it red.

His mark. Only temporary and yet, for some reason, she craved it. Craved more. A bite. A permanent claim.

A thought that should have scared her and it might have, only his mouth found hers for a torrid kiss full of lashing tongue and panted breaths.

He returned to her breasts, lavishing more attention on them, giving her a mini orgasm, a first from breast play alone. She hung onto that tiny climax as his mouth latched onto a nipple for a good hard sucking. She trembled as his tongue danced around the tip. She clenched hard inside when he switched nipples and started over.

His lips found hers again. And she kissed him. Hard. He didn't flinch. She nipped at his mouth hard enough he growled, but then again, he tugged her lips with his own teeth.

Passion getting out of hand?

Never.

When he broke off the kiss, she almost cried, only to hear his growled, "Time for honey."

She realized his intent. He kissed his way down, jawline to neck, down between the swell of her breasts and over her abdomen. He paused just above her curls, and by curls, she didn't mean a neatly trimmed tiny rosebud of a bush. She believed in being natural, and that meant curly, wild pubes.

Would he balk? It had happened before.

Edwina held her breath.

"I don't think I've ever wanted to taste something more in my life," he whispered as he drew close and breathed in her scent.

She couldn't help but clutch at his hair as he nuzzled her. He took his damned time, rubbing his cheek against her curls while his hands slid up her legs and held on to her thighs. He didn't need to part them. She'd already parked her ass on the island and spread them wide.

He chose to kiss her inner thighs rather than dive in.

She could have screamed.

He chose to cup her ass in his hands and draw her partially off the counter, supporting her as he leaned in to tease some more. He blew hotly on her nether region. Parted those lips with a finger, getting it slick on her honey. He sawed that finger over her clit, already sensitive. She bit her lip and moaned.

He dipped that finger inside, and she gasped.

He went back to teasing her clit.

Then in.

She held on to his shoulders as he teased her, his hot breath, his finger, and then his tongue. She almost came when he finally began licking as he thrust two fingers into her. She gripped him, and her heels dug into the edge of the counter as she held on to the pleasure humming throughout her body.

She was going to come, and hard if he kept it up. She couldn't be that selfish. "Now." She huffed as he flicked his tongue.

"Come for me, Honeybear," he commanded.

"But—" Shouldn't he want his pleasure, too?"

"Come for me," he whispered against her flesh.

He thrust a third finger into her, pushing hard as his teeth nibbled her clit.

She did as he asked and came. Hard. Wetly. As in holy honey. And did he care? Nope, that man hummed against her as he kept licking and finger fucking her to—

"Aaaah." She screamed as she rolled into the behemoth of orgasms. Wave after wave of pure bliss rocked her body.

And still he kept going, making her moan. "Enough. Your turn." Because that good turn deserved another.

She sat up and reached for his pants, the loose fabric giving her easy access to a shaft that promised a better ride than the vibrator in her bedroom.

She hopped off the island and shoved him against it. "Hold still while I drizzle some honey."

Before she could grab the dipper, the rumble of an approaching engine distracted her.

Just the plow. A plow that appeared to be headed up her driveway judging by the lights shining through her window.

He leaned back and said, "It appears we have company."

"Get dressed." She flew to the loft to fling on some clothing. As she tried to find the hole for her head, there was a pounding at her door and a bellowed, "We've come to rescue the prince!"

CHAPTER TEN

ON THE WORSE DAY OF CHRISTMAS, THE BIATCHES GAVE ME TO ME — SOME EPIC COCK BLOCKING.

Felix almost roared at the interruption. The only reason he didn't kill the lionesses that came traipsing in with loud voices and even louder personalities was because he didn't want to peeve Edwina. She wasn't the type to tolerate machismo actions. Even as she'd very much enjoyed his manhandling of her parts.

A good thing he'd been aware and present during the event, or he'd have wondered if it had happened at all. She did her best to pretend he wasn't there as she bustled in the kitchen, finally popping those rolls into the oven. She smiled too widely at the women crowding her home, who surely smelled what they'd been up to but wisely didn't remark upon it.

"Who wants coffee?" asked by a much-too-bright Edwina.

"We'll handle the coffee. I'm sure you need a break after caring for His Highness." It was Luna—more accurately her belly—that pushed Edwina into a chair, a spectator in her own kitchen as the women who'd braved the wintery conditions took over.

Reba handled the caffeine portion while the buns cooked. Luna whipped up a batch of pancake batter while Joan sizzled bacon and sausage. During all that inane chatter, he caught the gist of matters.

Apparently, Arik hadn't been pleased at all that the women of his Pride had forgotten his dear cousin and demanded they fetch Felix.

"...so we tried to make the trip in my SUV, but all wheel drive isn't so good when there are drifts more than a foot high." Reba scowled. "I'll be having a talk with my dealer about trading it in."

"Then Leo wouldn't loan us his truck," Joan grumbled. "Claims we would have caused damage."

"Which is kind of a dumb thing to say," Luna chimed in. "Because why else have a push bar unless you're going to actually push stuff with it!"

"Exactly what I said," Joan exclaimed.

Reba snorted. "You know how men are with their toys. You should have seen my mate's face when I asked to borrow the flame thrower."

That led to Edwina asking, "Why does he have a flame thrower?"

"Let's just say my man likes to be prepared for all kinds of possibilities." Reba's lips curved.

"So how did you make it?" Felix almost regretted asking.

"Well, I wanted to snowmobile in, only the one place within walking distance that sells them was closed on account of no power and we couldn't get to the other one. Hence why we commandeered a snowplow and came to the rescue," declared Luna, who really shouldn't be out of the city, given she could pop at any moment.

"Won't that cause trouble with the authorities?" Edwina queried.

"Our king demanded we rescue you. He can deal with the fines." Reba waved off the minor matter of possible theft.

"And here we are. At last. You're welcome." Joan beamed at him.

What did she have to be happy about? The fact his balls might just explode?

"Is it just me, or does he look peeved we're here? Were we interrupting something?" Luna asked a tad too sweetly.

Three sets of eyes swiveled between Edwina and Felix. He opened his mouth to snap yes, only to have Edwina jump up and say, "The cinnamon rolls are ready."

The next little bit involved eating, the Pride biatches dominating the conversation. He didn't get a chance to talk to Edwina, other than purr as he passed her taking his dishes to the sink, "Tastiest thing I've ever had in my mouth."

The blush in her cheeks showed she caught the

innuendo. She turned away and mumbled, "I'll send you back with the leftovers."

Those words acted as a cue for the lionesses to help with the cleanup. Reba also ordered him to pack up his stuff.

What stuff? Those useless and uncomfortable boots he'd bought for a thousand dollars that hurt his feet? He really didn't want to swap the soft plaid shirt for the scratchy wool one he'd arrived in. However, what choice did he have?

Edwina didn't ask him to stay, and he had too much pride to admit he'd rather not go. He needed an excuse. Something to keep him here that didn't involve him blurting out that he and Edwina had unfinished business.

As he tried to think up an excuse, he put on his uncomfortable clothes, his skin protesting the change in softness. He tamed his finger—ahem, passion—rustled hair and debated putting it in a bun just to get a rise out of Edwina.

In the end, he tugged it back into a loose tail and emerged from the bedroom he'd been using to see Edwina at the sink, back to him. She stiffened when he entered the main area but didn't turn around.

As he wedged his feet into the trendy boots, wincing as they pinched, Edwina neared, looking at everyone but him.

"Thanks for coming out," she said, handing over a tin with the promised rolls.

"We should thank you. Always wanted to drive one of those suckers," Luna exclaimed. The door opened, letting in a blustery draft that brought a shiver.

Edwina met his gaze for a second when she stepped forward with the coat he'd been using. She thrust it at him and said, "Keep this. You need this more than my grandpa does in Florida."

"Oh hell yeah," he muttered without thought as he reached for it. There was something to be said for the battered army green canvas with pockets. So many pockets, including two on the inside. Even better it came down past his butt and kept his back from getting a chill. Apparently, he'd reached that age in life where he noticed it. Comfort over style. He might be able to get used to this.

A distracted Joan and Reba balanced Luna as she put on her boots.

"Thank you for everything," he murmured, placing his hand on her arm when she would have moved away.

"It's nothing. Merry Christmas."

The reminder of the holiday had him grasping at excuses. "We can't leave Edwina here by herself. She still has no power."

"Not true. I've got a generator," the unhelpful ursine stated.

"Which doesn't help you with the Barry problem," he retorted.

"Who's Barry?" asked Joan.

"Her ex-boyfriend. He broke into her barn last night."

"Did you kill him? Need help getting rid of the body?" Luna asked, wedging her foot, after much stomping, into the boot.

"No." Not for lack of wanting, a part Felix kept to himself. Mother would skin him if he suddenly got the reputation of being a killer. She preferred he be discreet in his actions.

"Do you want us to make him disappear?" Luna breezily offered.

"That's really not necessary," Edwina interjected.

"It's not a problem. Pounding on something might help get this baby out." A claim that led to Luna glaring at her hump.

Edwina shook her head. "Barry's an idiot, but he doesn't need to die."

"He was after something. He might return," Felix argued.

"Doubtful, but even if he does come back, I'll handle it. Starting with new locks and an alarm on the barn door."

"Given how far your nearest neighbors are, you should install some motion cameras." Felix's many apartments in Europe, along with the family castle, had up-to-date security to keep the Spain Pride safe.

Edwina shook her head. "I don't trust those things. What if someone hacks them and sees something they shouldn't?"

A good point and why many shifter packs, sleuths, and prides eschewed their use. But only because they were lazy and cheap. "You make sure the footage is stored on a secure server that only you and those you trust can access."

"Pass. Sounds more complicated than it's worth."

"Come on, your furriness, time to bring you back the city." Luna tugged at his arm.

He'd run out of arguments, but despite that, he glanced at Edwina. She could stop his departure with a simple word.

She waved good-bye.

Joan slung an arm around Edwina. "If it makes you feel better, your prince-li-ness, I'll hang out and help reinforce security. Now that the road is plowed, someone can fetch me later, and we can keep swapping biatches in and out until we know this Barry fellow isn't coming back."

He had no excuses left. Tell the feet that refused to move.

He was given no choice. Luna belly checked him on her way out the door. He hit the stoop and had no choice but to stumble outside and then dodge the fetal hump looking to finish him off.

Framed in the doorway, Edwina said nothing. Then again, what was there to say?

They'd had some fun. Never made any promises. As to his desperation to stay? Blame his blue balls. He'd take care of it in a hot shower and be fine.

Reba and Luna squashed his ass between them on the front bench seat of the snowplow. Despite his reluctance, riding so high was actually kind of fun.

"Let's clear a path!" Luna uttered an evil chuckle when she lowered the blade and sheared snow onto the side of the road as they cleared their way back into the city, a city still digging itself out from the back-to-back storms. Sections of it remained without power, the streetlights dark, meaning people jostling for a turn through the intersections. They also had to play dodge the stuck cars. The main roads were mostly passable, but the side streets had vehicles buried and in need of serious help to get out.

They made surprisingly good time, mostly because Luna gunned at the cars in front of her, the plow's blade angled down. Would she actually sweep traffic aside? No one stayed in front to find out and split off so she could pass.

Terrifying, but fun.

Felix arrived at the condominium complex to find his cousin hanging in the common area by the decorated tree. Arik cut a fine figure despite the red sweater featuring some hideous Christmas scene that involved a nude Santa with a glass of milk positioned just right. He didn't appear to be the only one wearing an eyesore.

"Cousin! You're just in time!" Arik boomed. "We have a treat for you tonight."

"Hopefully not a matching sweater."

Arik grinned. "Isn't it hideous and amazing? Kira found it. I have one with a snowman upstairs you can borrow if you want."

"No, thanks. I'd rather not regret it in the morning. This treat, can it wait while I grab a shower and put on other clothes?"

"Thirty minutes. It's all I can give you. We wouldn't want to be late."

"Where are we going?"

"To the most amazing thing ever," Arik replied vaguely.

Intrigued, Felix quickly bathed, mostly to get the distracting scent of Edwina off his skin. The moment he did, he regretted it. However, his skin did thank him for the lotion and sucked it in greedily.

The coat she'd given him lay over a chair, and it occurred to him he'd seen the perfect hat to go with it. And he really needed better boots.

The sweater he changed into chafed, and he flung it aside looking for something a little more worn in. Someone shoot him. He already missed the plaid.

He settled on a long-sleeve Henley, burgundy for the holiday. He pulled his damp hair back and rejoined his cousin.

"Just in time. Prepare yourself for awesomeness." Arik slung his arm around Felix, and they walked a few blocks to a school. A stream of adults and children dressed in their best clothes—which ranged from full-on suits to jeans, white shirt, and clip-on tie for the boys, whereas most of the girls had stuck to either fancy dresses or Christmas gear that involved antlers.

"What insanity is this?" Felix breathed as he sat elbow to elbow in a gymnasium with undersized chairs. He spent the next three hours at a school Christmas concert where off-key younglings, including Arik's own cubs, sang with gusto.

Adorable.

For the first ten minutes.

After the first hour, he found himself drifting off, daydreaming of perfect children of his own standing on stage. Perfect miniature versions of him and—

"Edwina." Her name slipped from his lips as Felix startled awake.

Arik eyed him oddly. "What did you say?"

"Nothing." Because the very idea was crazy. Him and a bear? Not only would Mother never agree, he didn't see how it could work. He was a lion prince with a home in Europe. Edwina was a farmer who wore unmatching—ridiculously comfortable—clothes.

Totally unsuited.

So why did he miss her so much?

CHAPTER ELEVEN

ON TOO MANY DAYS BEFORE BEARMAS, THE LIONS GAVE TO ME – A REASON TO SELL MY FARM AND RELOCATE.

Edwina wanted to be alone, and yet it had been too many days since that happened. True to their word, the biatches took turns hanging out. Blame the prince who just had to blab about Barry.

The moment Simba and the two women left, Joan started. "Tell me about Barry."

"Nothing to tell. We met at a fair. I was selling Christmas bears and snowmen made from the leftover trunks of trees." She waved a hand to the one in the corner, two round slices for the body and head, smaller pieces for ears and paws, then painted with big round eyes. People paid big bucks for the simple Christmas art, and Edwina had fun making them.

"Did you sell honey, too?"

"Yeah. A few jars, given I had the business cards for the tree farm with me. Can't have a place called Honey Pine Farm and not actually have any honey."

"I assume while you dated he came to the house?"

"Once." Only after her family left. Given she knew he'd only be temporary, no point in them meeting.

"Felix seemed to think he was after something."

"Can't have been all that big seeing as how he came on snowmobile."

"He doesn't know about your other side?"

"Of course not. He's much too human, and I knew he wasn't the one." For some reason her mind veered to Felix. The way he'd kept flashing her grins that first day they'd shoveled snow. He tried to keep up and was such a good sport when he lost.

A man who kept his word and honored his bets. She took a sip of coffee to counter the tingle at the reminder.

"Maybe he was scouting."

"To do what? Steal my hives? These aren't thoroughbred horses."

"But your bees make super special honey."

"With guidance." Left unsaid was it also included the addition of a few extra ingredients that were a family secret.

"Someone stealing them might not know that."

"So what are you suggesting I do? Turn my barn into Fort Knox?"

"No, but we can make a few improvements." Joan winked. "Don't worry. Melly's husband is ordering the parts we need. He'll bring them over shortly and help us install them."

Edwina might have protested more, but the human Melly mated, a man called Theo, proved useful when it came to adding security to her barn. New locks. A solar-powered alarm. And despite her misgivings, Edwina allowed the installation of three cellular trail cams designed for hunters. The discreet units detected motion and sent the images to an app on her phone. They placed three on the property: one watching the woods, the other the road, and the third inside the barn itself.

That first night after Felix left, hearing the bed downstairs creak as Joan got comfortable, Edwina missed the darned prince. Missed a guy she hadn't even slept with. A pity they'd been interrupted before she could give him a ride. He had an endowment to put that stallion shifter she'd dated to shame. But it was for the best. Getting involved with a cat? It wouldn't end well for her. After all, Simba had only been at her place because he was stuck. If given the choice, he'd have immediately left.

So why had he appeared reluctant to depart?

Apparently, it passed because he didn't return. Flirty Joan got replaced by Nexxie then Reba who showed up for an overnighter with her spooky husband, Gaston. Luna also spent a few hours bitching about how the baby was never moving out and it was all her mate's fault. Said mate got told to sit in the car if he was going to just hover.

Finally, on the tenth day before Bearmas, Edwina

had enough of cats shedding all over the place and getting into her things. She wanted peace and quiet. She loaded up her most recent biatch—easier than expected once Edwina dangled some honey-flavored cotton candy in front of Meena's sensitive nose. Using the treat as bait, Meena climbed into the front seat of Edwina's truck. Edwina then insisted on driving her back to the city.

"Are you sure? I can stay. Leo loves spending time with the twins. And I'm sure those gray hairs that keep popping up are just a fluke. Even if they're not, I think my pookie looks distinguished, don't you?"

"Totally sexy," Edwina muttered, only to swerve as Meena growled, "Keep your paws off my mate, bear!"

"Not interested in him."

"Rumor has it you're into a prince," was Meena's sly reply.

"Bah. As if I'd date someone so vain. You should hear him go on and on about his hair."

"In his defense, he has nice hair. Soft to the touch," Meena mulled aloud—and almost got mauled for it. Edwina tightened her hands on the steering wheel instead of asking if Meena knew this from experience. She had no right to jealousy.

"I hear his mom wants him to get married." Meena continued talking about Felix.

Through gritted teeth, Edwina replied, "I'm sure she has some nice feline picked out for him."

"Doesn't matter what she thinks. The heart wants

what the heart wants. I predict when the prince falls in love, he won't care a whit about anything else. He will sweep his mate off her feet, and they'll live happily ever after in his castle."

"Sounds drafty," Edwina mumbled because she knew full well no one would ever sweep her into the air. She'd more likely give someone a slipped disk trying. She'd put on a bit of winter weight, as she did every year. Although it had been taking longer and longer in spring to shed it.

When they arrived at the condo, Edwina carried in a box of treats for the grownups while Meena held the box of honey lollipops for the cubs. By design, Edwina should add.

The moment Meena entered, the chaos of running children froze. Their heads swiveled as one. Their eyes flashed, intent hunters who'd caught a scent.

One of them growled, "Candy."

It acted as a call to action. The cubs charged Meena, whose eyes widened as she stopped sucking the lolly she'd snared from the box she wisely chose to drop.

Not a moment too soon, as the cubs swarmed it, laughing and jostling, smartly only grabbing one each under the watchful eye of parents who would chastise if they didn't share nicely—and by chastise Edwina knew that whoever showed greed would see their own treat confiscated and eaten in front of them. A few older siblings brought treats to those contained in strollers or strapped to a person.

While they were distracted, Edwina sidled sideways to get past them so she could drop her load of honey fudge for the adults. She'd no sooner set it down than awareness prickled her nape. She whirled to see Felix, looking distinguished in his trousers and button-up shirt, his golden hair perfectly coiffed. A prince once more.

"Hi," she muttered, feeling distinctly underdressed given she had on her candy cane leggings and Grinch sweater. Add in her almost knee-high pink Bog boots and her puffy winter jacket, she totally oozed sexy.

Not.

There would be no more passionate kisses. He'd returned to his world and senses.

"I didn't know you were coming," Felix exclaimed.

Why would he? It wasn't as if he called to ask her schedule. She didn't say that aloud and stuck to, "Just dropping off Meena then heading back."

"Oh." He almost sounded disappointed. "How are you?"

"Good. You?" Most awkward conversation ever.

Squeals showed cubs high on natural honey sugar once more racing around, a few trying to climb the tree, the goal being to not dislodge ornaments or else they'd get in trouble.

Felix winced at a particularly strident screech. "Want to go somewhere quiet for a coffee?"

She should say no. "Hell yes."

He grabbed her by the hand and tugged her back out the door into the chilly afternoon air.

She glanced at the sky then him. He had no jacket. "You'll freeze."

"We're not going far."

Indeed, the coffee shop sat right across the street and appeared full. Not that Felix let that stop him from weaving between the tables until he found one just vacated. He angled her into a chair with instructions. "Guard this spot while I get us hot cocoa."

Bemused, she watched as the prince stood in line, ignoring the giggles and admiring glances of the women in line with him. He ordered a pair of drinks and returned, the mugs he balanced showing off melting marshmallows atop the hot beverage. He set them down with an apologetic, "They had no honey."

She shuddered. "As if I'd eat store-bought, mass-produced junk."

He burst out laughing. "You sound like me and my hair products."

The comparison tilted her lips. "Guess we're both a little picky when it comes to certain things."

"Speaking of things, how's the farm?"

"Noisy."

Concern pulled his lips into a bow. "No one mentioned there'd been trouble."

Wait, did that mean he'd been checking in on her?

Why ask the lions when he could have called or texted?

"My problem is more along the lines of nonstop guests. I know the biatches mean well, but they never shut up."

"Right?" he exclaimed. "I'm debating getting earplugs and carrying them around."

"A sound plan. Me, I finally got desperate and lured the last lioness into my truck and drove her back to town. I can't wait to enjoy the silence."

"Lucky. I miss the peace of your home."

The admission surprised. "Don't you mean you miss your castle?"

"Nope. I actually found your place more relaxing." He shrugged as he added, "There was a time I really loved the royal life. Always going somewhere, constantly striving to look my best."

"And now?"

"It's tiring. I've never been more at ease than when we sat in your living room by the stove, reading about bees."

He made it sound nice, and yet, there was a flip side to it. "It can be lonely at times," she admitted. Then realized it might make her sound whiny and pathetic.

"Being a prince can be like that, too."

"How can you be lonely when you have people all around?"

"Strangers looking to get something from me, not

me as a person but me as a prince. It can be very isolating."

"Oh, the poor prince," she mocked, and just like at the farm, they fell into the same easy conversation and comradery they'd discovered before. Their chat lasted long enough it got dark outside.

"I should get going." She stood from the table.

"Do you have to?"

"I need to pack. I leave for Florida soon."

"I know… It's just…" The usually brash prince appeared at a loss for words. "It was so nice seeing you."

"Maybe we'll cross paths again one day." A lame reply, especially since it would be unlikely.

"Edwina—"

She paused halfway to the door.

Whatever he meant to say got wiped as a crew of biatches entered, squealing, "We need hot cocoa. Stat!"

"Bye, prince," Edwina said softly, turning to go. To her surprise, he spun her back around, having closed the distance between them.

"What are you doing?" she gasped.

"What I've been thinking about since we parted." He kissed her.

Soundly.

It led to much cheering and hot cheeks on her part. Before she could escape, the ladies of the Pride invited —and by invited she meant they demanded—Edwina join them for dinner at the Pride-owned restaurant nearby.

She would have said no, but Felix leaned close and said, "Please. I don't want you to go quite yet."

How could any woman say no?

The restaurant proved noisy and boisterous, but the food was excellent. As for the company, she could find no fault with Felix. He was charming. Attentive. And distracting as heck.

When she excused herself for the washroom it was more to splash water on her flushed face than anything else. When she returned to the table, Felix stood out of respect, his gaze unwavering on her, despite her hideous outfit.

Someone yelled, "Mistletoe."

Edwina tilted her head, and she saw the sprig being held above her and Felix by a grinning Meena. The lioness waggled the stick she'd tied it to. "You have to kiss. It's the law."

Edwina might have protested, only Felix leaned in with a whispered, "We wouldn't want to be breaking any rules."

The press of his mouth to hers made her forget everything.

Who he was. Where they were. Nothing existed but the heat that ignited between them. It lasted too long and not long enough. They sat down to drunken cheering, and Meena moved on to other couples with her mistletoe.

The damage was already done, though. The fire inside her didn't go out, and when Felix brushed his mouth against her ear after dessert with a murmured, "Spend the night," there was only one thing to say.

"Okay."

CHAPTER TWELVE

ON THE EVE BEFORE CHRISTMAS, A BEAR GAVE TO ME – HERSELF.

Felix wanted to toss Edwina over his shoulder and run back to the condo and the guest suite assigned to him. A part of him worried Edwina would change her mind. However, they made it past the door to his temporary place. Just in time.

Clothes went flying, hitting the floor in untidy heaps, and he didn't care.

Their lips locked, and that was all that mattered.

He'd not realized how badly he'd wanted this—Edwina in his arms—until he had her. Now he would quench that thirst.

Their hands made quick work of their clothes, and he didn't care if his expensive shirt wrinkled on the floor or that he ripped his damned snug jeans yanking them off. He needed to feel his skin on her. He stroked her bared flesh, his hands skimming down her back to the swell of her ass. She cupped his face and kissed him, her tongue inside his mouth where he could suck it.

He pushed her against the wall of the condo, and she hiked a leg around his haunches, all the better to give him access to her sex. He dipped a finger into her honey pot, feeling the heat, the wetness, the quiver of her excitement.

He thrust a second finger into her, and she clutched at him, gasping, "Yes. Give it to me."

"I will when I'm good and ready. First, I need to taste you again."

Because he'd been unable to forget the flavor of her. Craved it more than anything he'd ever encountered. And he would have it again.

The bare wood floor would kill his knees, so he scooped her into his arms, ignoring her soft protest. "Put me down. You'll break your back."

Rather than reply, he kissed her. She sighed into his mouth, and he got the pleasure of carrying her to his bed.

And, yes, it was a pleasure. To have her in his arms. Her scent enveloping him. Her hands touching. Lips kissing.

She lay on his mattress, and he covered her, his body pressing down on hers as his mouth remained latched to hers, their tongues dueling. His throbbing cock was pinned between their bodies.

But he wanted more.

He broke the kiss only so he could do other things

with his mouth. He parted her thighs that he might get between them and watched her as his fingers found her button and teased it. Her hips arched off the bed. She gasped. Panted.

Wanted...

As he kept fingering her, he let his tongue finally taste that honey. As delicious as he recalled, he hummed as he lapped, hardened when she came, her sex clenching tight around his fingers, pulsing in waves.

And still he kept teasing her, building that frenzy into an even tauter need. One that had her dragging him so that she could kiss his mouth. Her hands dug into his buttocks as she spread herself wide enough to accommodate his frame.

"Don't keep me waiting," she growled when he only teased her sex with the head of his cock.

"As my Honeybear commands." He thrust into her and was almost undone. She clenched him so tight he might never escape.

Just fine with him since he'd found true heaven.

Together they rocked and thrust. Rolled their hips and panted for air. Passion ruled them both, a wild thing that didn't end when they both orgasmed.

Even when the sweat cooled and their heart rates slowed, they clung to each other.

Their second bout ended up less frantic and just as intense.

A shower led to round three and Felix calling for food, because a well-sexed ursine apparently needed snacks. Then, despite the fact she had no honey on hand, she went down on him, and he roared. Loud enough someone pounded at the door.

"You okay in there?"

Shifter hearing meant he heard a second person shushing the first with a not-so-quiet, "Can't you see he's getting it on with someone?"

Not just a someone.

His Honeybear.

Mine.

They fell asleep entwined, his boneless body draped over hers. The fact he covered her like a blanket was the only reason he woke when she tried to slip out from under him and disturbed his rest.

"Where are you going?" he murmured drowsily as she left the bed.

"Home."

Given he'd expected her to say potty, that rather surprised him. His eyes fully opened, and he rolled to see her. "Home? But it's late." Or early, depending on how someone viewed it.

"Less traffic this time of night. Or should I say morning, seeing as how it's an hour 'til dawn."

"Stay." Apparently he wasn't averse to begging.

She bit her lower lip and gave it some thought before shaking her head. "I can't. My flight leaves in a few hours, and I still haven't packed or prepped the house for when I'm gone."

"But..." A jumble of words hovered on the tip of his tongue—*Stay with me. Be mine. Love me...*

Rather than say the wrong thing, he said nothing at all.

And she left. Left him on Christmas Eve.

Worst present ever.

CHAPTER THIRTEEN

ON THE DAY BEFORE BEARMAS, MY TRUE LOVE GAVE TO ME — NOTHING. BECAUSE HE TURNED OUT TO NOT BE MY LOVE, I GUESS.

Despite the pleading in his eyes, Edwina left the vain prince who turned out to be not so vain and a better lover than she'd have expected. Not selfish one bit given he'd been all about her pleasure.

And what pleasure he'd given.

She'd never come so hard. Never squeezed someone so tight without breaking them. He'd not squeaked once in pain. Rather, the more she unleashed, the more aroused he became. She'd actually made him roar. A first for her, and kind of awesome.

When he asked her to stay, she almost said yes. The thought of spending the day in his arms really had her wondering why she'd chosen to get in a cold truck and drive home on roads that were barely passable in some cases. Yet here she was, straining to see, steering carefully, and sometimes defensively when the back end of her vehicle slipped.

The excuse she'd used, a plane ticket, sounded so lame. Yes, she was supposed to fly out to meet her parents and grandfather, but if she called and said she'd decided to wait a few extra days because she'd met someone, her mother would totally understand and even encourage it. Mama had said more than once she wished Edwina could find someone so she wouldn't be alone. Didn't matter how many times Edwina claimed to not mind the solitude. Having met Felix, and knowing how her parents were with each other, she finally understood what she was missing.

A companion. A lover. What a pity that she'd come to that realization with a prince of all people. Doomed to failure from the start. He didn't belong here. No matter how much fun he had in her bed, eventually he would go home.

Without her.

Better to avoid that heartache and travel to Florida where she'd be fed fresh seafood by her mother, grilled on the business by her father, and entertained by stories of idiots by the eldest. She could even steal the remote from Grandpa for shits and giggles.

Her phone began buzzing on the final road into her place. Her old truck didn't have a built-in navigation system, and she wasn't dumb enough to try checking it while driving in the dark on possible black ice.

As she neared the entrance to her farm, she noticed a large cube van parked in her drive, silhouette outlined against the dawning sky. The headlights on it were bright, and she squinted as she angled to park at its side.

"What in the honey nut..." she muttered, swinging out of her truck. The roll-up door on the rear of the unmarked vehicle gaped in the direction of her barn.

Two burly guys exited the barn, carrying a hive.

"Excuse me, but what the hell do you think you're doing?" Edwina barked even as it appeared clear. She'd interrupted a honey heist!

"Don't get involved." Grunted by the low-browed neanderthal on the left. In direct contrast his companion had a massive forehead and thinning hair that he valiantly kept in long, greasy strands.

Edwina crossed her arms over her chest. "I will get involved because that's my barn you're robbing."

"Whatever, lady. Got a problem? Talk to the guy who hired us."

"Wait, someone hired you?" she repeated dumbly, only to clue in a second before Barry, the culprit and obvious mastermind of this stupidity, sauntered from the barn. "Just what do you think you're doing?" she snapped.

"A better question is, why are you here? Shouldn't you be flying to your parents like you do every year?"

"My flight isn't until later."

"My bad. I assumed from the truck missing overnight that you were gone." Indicating he'd been watching.

"And you thought you could rob me?" She shook her head. "Not a good idea."

"Who's going to stop me? The cops are too far out. And I'll bet you didn't even call them."

He'd be right. "You'll go to jail for this."

"No one will know it's me. Did you really think I was stupid and wouldn't notice the cameras? I wore a face covering until we destroyed the pair."

Pair? That meant he didn't know about the third one. Not that it helped. Edwina insisted on keeping the farm's security footage private, meaning the police didn't get an automated call when the cameras detected motion, and neither did a security firm.

But in good news, with the cameras gone, she could eat Barry's face. So long as she washed away the blood after she got rid of the body—make that three bodies—she'd be fine.

Not her first choice. She really hated flying on a full meat belly.

"Surely there are easier cons than stealing my hives. You do realize, even with my bees, you still need fields and flowers, plus, do you have a bottling system?"

The more she asked questions, the tighter his expression. "I don't give a shit about the honey other than I heard someone in the bar say you were sitting on liquid gold. I need money fast, and since your house doesn't have anything of worth other than some junk jewelry, I'm going to sell your bee boxes."

"To who?"

"I'll find someone. Maybe your rival will want it."

The only rivalry she indulged in was at the fair. Everyone knew her honey was not only better quality than *Honey-dils*, Edwina sold it for half the price.

"You are messing in things you don't understand." She stiffened as the carrying duo came down the truck ramp and headed into the barn.

"This is all your fault, you know. Dumping me like you did, and after I was so nice to you. You should have been appreciative."

"Of what?" she asked because she truly had to wonder.

"The fact I pretended to not care you're Sasquatch-sized."

She glanced down at herself. No, she'd never be delicate or dainty or petite. At the same time, she didn't have confidence issues when it came to her looks. She was attractive to the right kind of guy. Like Felix.

A man she'd left in a warm bed for this shit. She rubbed her forehead. "You will tell your thugs to put my hives back, and maybe, just maybe, I can be convinced to forget I ever saw you. Think of it as a Christmas present you don't deserve."

"You're not the one calling the shots," Barry blustered. "I'm not going anywhere, and neither are you."

"Is that supposed to be a threat? I know you. You're not going to hurt me." She went to move past Barry, and he grabbed her by the arm tight enough it would leave a bruise.

She eyed the hand on her body then him. "I wouldn't do that if I were you."

"Or what?"

"Or I might just remove it and smack you with it," she growled.

"Big words for someone without a gun," Barry drawled, pulling one from his waistband.

Idiot. She batted it out of his hand.

His gaze narrowed. "I'm tired of you not taking me serious."

"Ditto. Guess I should have warned you sooner not to poke the bear."

"You giant fucking cow. Stop trying to emasculate me."

"Oh, is little Barry feeling inadequate? I'm surprised at your age that still happens given you had decades to come to grips with your lack of size." She dropped her gaze. No need to be subtle. It had been part of the reason they didn't last too long. She shouldn't have to ask, "*Are you in?*"

"Apologize." He lunged, and she side-stepped with a laugh.

"You'll have to be faster than that."

"No, I just needed to distract you." The smirk was too late of a warning. As she whirled, she saw his hired goons behind her; one of them held a taser.

No big deal. A big girl could handle a bit of electricity.

The zap hit her flesh, stronger than expected, and

she grunted, her teeth clacking together hard. She hit the ground on her knees as it kept jolting her. Still, she might have been okay if not for the second jab. Apparently, Barry didn't have just a gun in his pocket. As he added to the electrocution, she hit the ground jiggling.

By the time Barry and company dragged her into the woods, amidst a lightly falling snow, she'd lost consciousness.

CHAPTER FOURTEEN

ON THE EVE BEFORE CHRISTMAS, MY SUBCONSCIOUS GAVE TO ME—AN IDEA WORTHY OF A ROMANTIC COMEDY.

After Edwina left, Felix stayed in bed. What was the point of getting up? It wasn't as if he had anywhere to go. Anyone to see. Edwina had exited his life as quickly as she entered.

And that made this prince sad.

Admittedly, he didn't know Edwina as a person very well, not yet. But he wanted to. The glimpses he'd seen so far made him realize he wanted to spend more time with her. On the farm, where they could bask in those peaceful moments. In bed, where her passion delighted. Over a coffee, where they could talk and talk about real things and not fluff—*Is it true you sleep on a bed with gold sheets?* After reading about honeys, the scientist in him had some ideas. Ideas he wanted to share with someone who would understand.

Edwina.

But getting to know her meant not returning home.

It wasn't as if he were urgently needed in Spain. As a matter of fact, given the company's expanding business, they would be opening a satellite office somewhere in this city and required someone to run it.

Why not him? He could spearhead the expansion. Get himself an office building. But rather than living in the Pride condo owned by his cousin, perhaps he could commute from a farm.

If a certain bear said yes to dating a prince.

A bear about to get on a plane while he moped in bed.

If only he could have had this revelation before she left. Now he'd have to wait until she returned.

Sadness. Even his hair wilted with regret. It called for coffee and donuts, the effect on his gut be damned. It took but a second to order from the coffee shop, and the ridiculous tip he added ensured it got to his door in under fifteen minutes. Only then did he drag his ass out of bed.

Felix chugged his super-sized caramel mocha latte while noshing on sugar-dipped pastries and barely listened to the news.

"...flights cancelled due to the storm."

Wait, what did he hear? The newscast moved on rather than repeat. Felix glanced outside his window at the gray sky and falling snow. More snow on top of the slushy mess not yet cleared, making the sloppy streets even more treacherous, and grounding planes in the process.

"What a beautiful day!" he yelled, because the horrible weather kept Edwina on the ground, which meant he still had a chance.

He thought of texting her—*Hey Honeybear, I see your flight got delayed, want some company?*—but that seemed trite. Asking Edwina to give him a chance, to allow him to be her partner in life, called for a grand gesture.

"I shall tell her how I feel in person." For that, he had to get to Honey Pine Farm.

A plan quickly foiled.

Forget a rental or even hired conveyance. Christmas Eve was too busy on the best of days; add in a snowstorm with sloppy conditions and the roads were at a standstill

Felix paced the lobby as yet another car service, despite the money he promised, said it would be hours before they could accommodate.

"What's wrong? You look like someone stole your tiara," Luna remarked, her deadly belly angled in his direction.

"First off, I wear a crown, which is currently locked in a safe." Mother put it in time-out when he and his sister spatted over who should get to wear it. "I'm pissed because your weather sucks and the roads are impassable."

"No shit. It's winter. You need to go somewhere?"

Pride wouldn't help Felix get to Edwina. He needed help. "I have to get to Honey Pine Farm."

"Why?" Luna's eyes widened. "Oh. My. GAWD." She whirled, cupped a hand to her mouth, and bellowed, "Operation Honey Prince is a go."

"What?" Felix asked as suddenly biatches popped up out of everywhere. Hidden under couches, behind potted plants. One even dropped from a vent overhead.

Soon he was surrounded by jubilant biatches, the most frightening kind.

"I knew it. She's his mate!" Reba jabbed a finger in his direction. "Took you long enough to figure it out."

"I. Uh." The suave prince stumbled.

"I saw it the moment she sniffed in disdain at his stupid boots." Nexxie sighed. "So romantic. We should get those suckers bronzed."

"I'll bet it was his huge dick." Silence fell after Joan's words. The woman got indignant and huffed, "You don't have to eyeball me like that. Just because I prefer pussy doesn't mean I don't notice these things. Where do you think I get my dildo design ideas from?"

There was way too much to unwrap in that statement, so Felix avoided it and focused on the important thing. "Can you get me to Edwina so I can talk to her?"

"Talk. Ha." Joan slapped him on the back. "Are you going to have the same kind of talk like you did last night?"

"Holy catnip on a cracker, that was them?" Melly exclaimed. Once again, Felix became the focus of too many eyes.

"If we'd known you were a screamer, we'd have put

you in the guest suite across the road. Some of us like our sleep uninterrupted." A grumble by Luna.

"Leave the poor guy alone. I think we all remember what it's like when we first fall in love." Meena sighed, hand to her chest. "Leo had to put our mattress on the floor after we broke that third bed frame in a week."

Love? "I never said I, uh, loved her," Felix stammered.

"Why else would you be desperate to venture into a storm?" Nexxie pointed out. "It really is a Pridemas special. A foreign prince falls for the beekeeper and will do anything to reach her and declare his love."

"And they were mated happily ever after," Meena sang.

"So romantic." The group of biatches practically swooned.

Felix felt panic.

For a moment, his confidence left him. All his life he'd fought against ever being actually linked to someone. Fought settling down. Fought his mother's matchmaking.

Only because he'd not met Edwina. Love wasn't something he should fear, but rather embrace.

His shoulders went back. "None of that will happen unless I can talk to her. Edwina was supposed to be going to Florida for Christmas, but her flight was cancelled. I have to get to her farm, but the roads are a mess, and I can't find a ride."

Meena wrapped an arm around his upper body

and squeezed, causing a few ribs to protest. "Fear not, Prince. You've asked the right people to help."

"You still have the snowplow?" he asked, suddenly feeling hopeful.

"Bah. Forget that clunky, noisy thing." Reba grinned, a terrifying thing. "Since that escapade, we've had time to better equip ourselves. Biatches!" The voices all died as they listened to Reba. "Designated riders, gear up and head for the sleds."

The what?

Luna slapped his arm. "Go get some warm stuff on and meet us in the garage. We leave in five."

He might have argued, but by the sounds of it, they had a plan.

It involved five snowmobiles, shiny and new, parked on trailers. Melly already worked at the straps on one, while Meena worked on another. Luna stood to the side arguing with a man who made the mistake of pointing at her belly and saying, "Is that really wise?"

"Try and stop me and see what happens," Luna snarled.

"You're insane. But I love you," the man grumbled as he walked away, getting into an SUV that likely wouldn't make it far. But snowmobiles... Felix began to really admire the Pride biatches' style.

"I'm here. Which machine is mine?" he asked. He'd never driven one, but how hard could it be?

Luna pointed. "You're riding with Melly."

The petite woman grimaced as she put on her

helmet. "You better hope my hubby doesn't get jealous and freeze your bank account. You don't want to know what happened when some moose from Canada got drunk and flirted with me."

Nexxie leaned close and whispered, "Arrested at the border and cavity searched because of a tip."

"No one ever proved that was my mate," Melly argued.

Just in case, though, Felix hastened to say, "Can someone inform him I only want Edwina?"

His statement resulted in numerous happy sighs, ruined by a yelled, "Last biatch to the farm is rubbing my feet." Luna straddled her machine and shot off on her bright green machine.

Reba rode a red rocket, Meena got blue, Joan's was orange, and Melly, with the only passenger, had the yellow machine.

Their snowmobiles, loud grumbly beasts of metal and rubber track, rolled out of the garage, smoking enough that Felix didn't mind the hideous glittery helmet they gave him to wear. The moment they got outside and hit some snow the ride smoothed.

Somewhat. Apparently, the biatches thought Felix needed to get to the farm quickly, and not necessarily alive. He hung on for dear life as they weaved the snowy streets, using the road when they could, the sidewalk when they couldn't. The few pedestrians still trying to shop last minute in the storm mostly got out of the way. Smart on their part, given the cackling pregnant woman in the oversized parka and helmet labelled Super Biatch who yelled, "Move or you'll get stitches for Christmas."

What people must think looking out their window and seeing them careening about he didn't dare wonder and hoped they chalked it up to really good eggnog. The spiked kind that he should be lapping in front of a roaring fire instead of holding on to Melly, praying her husband wasn't ruining his finances, as they took turns so sharply they almost tipped over.

The ride become somewhat less chaotic as they left the city, racing down the snowy highway, swooshing around the stranded cars. Despite the shortening of the miles between him and Edwina, his anxiety didn't lessen.

Wait, was he worried she wouldn't be happy to see him? Everyone loved seeing him. Mostly. What if she wasn't? Would his sudden arrival come across as clingy?

He refused to let such doubts fester. Doubt brought anxiety. Anxiety caused wrinkles.

He had to trust in what he felt for Edwina. Hope she felt it, too. And if she didn't, then he'd prove to her —and himself.

The snow kept falling, a delicate flutter of flakes that was quite pretty even as it covered everything in a fluffy blanket of white. It reminded him of the first storm when he'd gotten snowed in with Edwina.

Maybe he'd get luck, and they'd be trapped again together. Wouldn't that be a special present?

Shit. A present. In his rush to reach her, he'd forgotten to get her anything.

Too late now.

Not far from the farm, a snowmobile died. Meena slapped at it, but that didn't give it more gas.

It was Melly who grumbled, "I thought these tanks were full."

"They were, but we might have taken a couple out for test rides." Meena's lips turned down.

"Double up," Reba ordered with a clap of her hands.

By the time the third sled died from lack of fuel, they'd reached the entrance to the farm. Felix still held on to Melly, who followed Luna, theirs the only two machines still—

Cough. Luna's engine ceased running.

Being a gentleman, Felix jumped off and offered his spot to Luna, who smacked his hand. "I'm pregnant, not useless."

Still, he couldn't ride while Luna and her belly walked. Melly came to the same conclusion, and the trio continued their trudge to the main part of the yard and the house.

As they travelled, Felix noted the driveway hadn't been cleared at all and showed partially snowed-in ruts. Big fat ones that didn't come from Edwina's truck. They found it parked at a strange angle beside a large rectangular spot that looked as if something had been parked when the snow started and then moved.

"The lights are off," he observed, heading for the house.

"Maybe the power is out again?" Melly offered.

"Maybe," he replied. What he didn't say? With the weather making things gloomy, Edwina would have lit candles and—he sniffed the air—it didn't smell like the stove was going. Had she left? Maybe gotten a ride to the airport before finding out she was grounded?

A firm knock netted no reply. Neither did the hard pounding. The door handle didn't turn when he gripped it.

She was gone. He was too late.

Melly yelled, "The barn door is open, and the hives are gone."

What?

Felix swung down off the porch and headed for the barn. "Any sign of Edwina?"

Melly shook her head. "No one's inside, and all her bee stuff is gone."

That wasn't Edwina's doing he'd wager. "We have to find her."

"I'm going to do a circuit around the house." Luna went to waddle off, but Felix stopped her.

"The snow's falling too hard. You'll never find a trail. And we don't want to lose you, too."

"Ah, Prince, I'm fond of you as well, but I'm taken." Luna patted his cheek.

Thank whatever lion god existed for that. Luna could be terrifying.

"Is it possible whoever stole the hives took Edwina?" Melly queried.

His mind flashed to Barry. The human was no match for Edwina alone, but what if he'd had help?

"Only one way to find out. The cameras you installed. They would have seen what happened. Can tell us who took her." As he spoke aloud, his excitement grew. "Melly, get your husband on the phone. We need access to the security footage."

Melly wrung her hands. "It's private. Only Edwina has access."

He crossed his arms and stared at her. "Like you didn't keep a backdoor." He knew the biatches well enough by now to guess.

"I kind of promised I wouldn't."

He kept staring.

She sighed. "Fine, I'll call Theo and tell him to take a peek. He won't be happy though, because that means letting Nexxie drive."

Apparently, Theo had swapped seats already because before Melly could call, her phone rang. Within seconds of her answering, judging by the expression on Melly's face, Felix expected bad news. Melly confirmed it by saying, "Edwina's in trouble."

Felix roared loud enough snow fell from nearby tree branches. Eventually he calmed enough to mutter, "What happened?"

Cameras One and Two caught a truck pulling into the farm early that morning. Then those cameras went dark. Camera Three, though, gave them a glimpse of two culprits, one of whom Felix recognized.

Barry. The prick had returned, and while they couldn't exactly see what he'd done to Edwina, there was video witness of her being dragged into the woods by Barry and someone else.

Two men dragged a limp woman in. Only two men came out.

She was still in the forest, and if alive, she needed his help.

No ifs. She had to be alive.

This was Felix's fault because he should have never let her go. He should have joined her on her trip. At the very least seen her safely home and to the airport. Shouldn't have been too proud to tell a fabulous woman just how much he admired her. How much he wanted to be with her.

How much he liked her hair.

"She's in the woods. I have to find her." Felix gave it no second thought, but the biatches tried to be the voices of reason for once.

"Don't be silly. Have you seen the weather? You'll get lost and die." Melly and her logic.

"Even I know better than to wander the woods when it's getting dark in a storm." Luna, the least responsible of them all, had something to say.

"How will you bring her out?" Melly basically insulted him by calling him weak.

"I'm not leaving her out there."

"Obviously. We just need a few minutes to find some gas to fill up the sleds. We don't have enough to go more than a few miles." Melly waved in the direction of their parked rides farther down the driveway. "I'll bring the machines to the barn while you guys find some gas. That will give time for everybody to show up so we can cover more ground." The walking biatches wouldn't be far behind.

Melly barked orders and left while Luna grumbled, "I've got gas, too much of it. If only we could use it for something other than making my husband turn green." Luna stomped in the direction of the barn.

What if she didn't find fuel? What if waiting proved the wrong choice?

Knowing they'd say no, Felix didn't ask. He set out on foot toward the forest where the camera last spotted Edwina. He wore the new boots he'd invested in guaranteed to keep his tootsies warm. He should have known when he went looking for the footwear that went high on his calf and could withstand the deepest cold that he wasn't going anywhere. Who spent an hour examining scarves and split mittens other than a man already subconsciously planning a return to a frigid farm? A good thing he'd gone shopping. It meant he was prepared to brave the elements.

As he entered the woods, he doubted he'd find a trail, but he wasn't about to give up.

His Honeybear had once braved a storm to save him.

He would do the same.

CHAPTER FIFTEEN

ON THE LAST DAY BEFORE CHRISTMAS, MY TRUE LOVE GAVE TO ME – A CHANCE TO BE A HERO.

The forest boughs did lessen the snowfall somewhat, but as it accumulated in the branches overhead, it contributed to the deepening gloom.

As suspected, no trail remained, nor even a scent, the outdoor air too crisp and sharp. Felix trudged on, wondering if he should yell or not. What if Edwina never replied because Barry had killed her?

No.

He refused to think that pissant managed to destroy Edwina. She was too brave and strong for that. She also knew these woods much better than him.

He paused and glanced around. Tree. More trees. Snow. More snow.

How would he ever find her?

"Honeybear! Where are you?" he bellowed.

Instead of her replying, he got a squirrel. It popped

its head out of the bole of a tree, wearing a red Santa hat, and chattered at him.

Felix stared at it before saying, "You! You're the squirrel who bombed me with an acorn." Annoying at the time but now... If not for the little guy, he'd have never gotten snowed in. "You're Rudy, right? Edwina told me about you."

The little fellow got excited and squeaked up a storm.

Which gave Felix an idea. "Hey, you know Edwina? I'm looking for her. Someone dragged her into these woods. I think she might be hurt."

"Chit-chat-chit." The squirrel went off again and even clutched its furry breast.

"I need your help. Help me find Edwina and I will personally deliver the biggest bag of nuts."

Now people often called non-shifting animals dumb. More like they couldn't be bothered. Unless you bribed them with food.

The pompom on Rudy's hat bounced as he chirped and held out his arms as wide as they could go.

"Even more nuts than that. A lifetime supply." Never mind the inanity of negotiating with a squirrel. He was desperate.

Rudy tweeted a high-pitched noise and clapped his paws.

"Do we have a deal?"

"Squeak." Rudy swung out of the burrow and

clambered down to a lower branch before waving his paws, obviously expecting to be carried.

"Just so we're clear, no more acorns to the head though."

He'd have sworn Rudy chuckled as he leapt to Felix's shoulder. The squirrel guided him, not alone he soon realized, as some of the chirps from Rudy resulted in replies that sometimes had the squirrel on his shoulder poking him to change direction.

By the time they located Edwina, Felix was well and truly lost. But he didn't care. He'd found her, curled in a ball in the snow, her clothes exploded around her bear body. Despite being unconscious, she'd shifted shapes to protect herself from the cold.

While Felix might not have much experience with ursine, he was familiar with the expression, "Don't wake a sleeping bear."

And she most definitely slept. Her chest rose and fell slowly, so very slowly, as her body preserved itself by falling into hibernation mode. Contrary to what she'd told him before, she didn't snore, although she did grumble the one night they spent together when he'd tried to move to the mattress so he didn't squish her. Apparently, she'd rather be squished, and as a feline, he liked to be the one doing the squishing.

He approached and ran a hand down her flank, reassured by the fact she lived, but now plagued with the problem of how to wake her without getting eaten. What if she'd been drugged or hibernated too deep?

Felix wasn't a weak man, but even he doubted he could drag her bear ass to safety.

Rudy had leapt from his shoulder to Edwina's body with no fear at all. Kind of reassuring.

Felix leaned back on his haunches and sighed. "Any suggestions on how to get her back to the farm?"

"Cheep," Rudy exclaimed and then leaped into a tree and bolted.

"Wait!" Felix yelled. While Rudy couldn't help carry Edwina, he'd been Felix's only hope to find his way out of the woods. But Rudy and his red cap were gone. The meager afternoon daylight waned, and despite his expensive and quality gear, the cold tried to seep in.

Only one thing to do. He snuggled into Edwina and murmured, "Come on, Honeybear, wake up."

Nothing, not even a twitch.

He reached a gloved hand out and stroked her furry cheek. "You know, I wasn't supposed to fall for an American bear. My mother will be most put out."

No reply.

"Too bad, because since meeting you, I can't stop thinking about you. You're positively splendid. Guess Mother will have to learn to live with it."

Hot air huffed against the top of his head, felt even through the hat messing up his hair.

"Edwina? Are you awake?" He angled enough to see she had an eye open. He grinned. "Thank goodness. I was about to give you great big ol' kiss if you didn't." After all, that always worked in the movies.

She shut her eyes, and he laughed. "Guess I need to wake my Honeybear."

He brushed his lips to her fur. "I'm glad you're okay." She might be, but he began to feel the cold and couldn't help a shiver.

She responded by wrapping him in a furry embrace.

It led to him grumbling, "I am supposed to be saving you."

Her body shook as if in mirth, and she nuzzled his head.

"Is this where I admit I'm lost? Rudy ran off, and I have no idea how to get us back."

She snuffled and then rolled to her side as if to stand, only she uttered a grunt of pain.

"What's wrong?" He quickly stood and had to circle to the side that had been plastered to the ground to see the jagged cut along her thigh. The blood had stained the snow under her.

"You're hurt!" The sight of it sent him into action. He unzipped his coat and tore a strip from his new—and guaranteed soft—plaid shirt.

She sat on her rump and cocked her head at the sight.

"What can I say? You converted me. I am now a man of comfort instead of the latest fashion."

"Chuff. Chuff."

"Don't get too cocky yet, my squishy Honeybear. I might be willing to change some things, but you will never get me to abandon my face cream. Although I have an idea to create a version with honey."

Could a bear hum happily? Because Edwina did as he talked to her and did his best to cover her wound. He had to give up. In her bear shape she had too much girth to wrap.

"Well, this is a dilemma. You're too injured to walk, and I can't carry you as a bear, but if you shift, you'll be naked which, granted, is a wonderful thing to behold; however, I don't want you getting frostbite. And if I give you my clothes, then I don't know how long I'll be able to carry you before I succumb to the frigid temperature."

She leaned on him in commiseration, and he almost fell over.

"What are we going to do, Honeybear?" They needed a Christmas miracle.

As if in reply to his wish, he heard the sudden jangle of bells.

What could it be?

Did it matter? He stood and yelled, "Over here."

The chime of bells soon turned into the blink of colorful lights that even the gloomy storm couldn't hide. The cause turned out to be the bright red sleigh he'd seen on Edwina's front lawn, the same one she'd used to pull trees. It came into view, solar-powered

Christmas lights wrapped harness-like around the seven lions and wolf pulling it.

He blinked, but still there were lions and a wolf barreling at him with the sleigh and guiding them with a red-hatted squirrel on her shoulder?

A very pregnant Luna, who pulled to a stop and grinned.

"Ho fucking ho. Need a ride?"

CHAPTER SIXTEEN

ON THE TWELFTH DAY OF BEARMAS, MY TRUE LOVE GAVE TO ME – A FAIRY TALE RESCUE.

Edwina couldn't believe her eyes. Her sleigh was being pulled by a lone wolf and lions—male and female alike—some of them wearing blankets she recognized as coming from her house to keep their flanks warm. Her outdoor lights gave them a merry brightness. The manes of the males in the group had frosted, giving them a certain flair.

Felix noticed her admiration and grumbled, "My mane is more impressive."

Everything about him was. Including the fact he'd risked his life coming to find her, which made her wonder why he was here in the first place. Only one way to find out.

She stood and shook her fur free of snow and ice then flipped into her skin that pimpled in the cold, but not for long. The lions had stocked the sled with blankets, a few sweaters, and socks. One of those sweaters, a plaid that Felix wore only a few days ago, ended up binding her leg. The scratch was long and ugly, but it would heal. Especially once she slathered some Honey-fix ointment on it.

While Luna tied off her leg and Rudy sat on Edwina's shoulder chattering away, Felix went around offering the waiting lion team a drink of cocoa from the thermoses they'd brought. Edwina gulped down some as well, feeling her slow and lumbering body waking. A little bit longer and she might not have woken up.

Felix tucked her into the sleigh, blankets all around. So nice and cozy, but nothing as warm as the man by her side.

A prince who'd come to her rescue.

"Giddyap, you hos and bros," Luna yodeled. The wolf gave her a dirty look, and Edwina snickered. Jeoff didn't appear happy with his mate. Rudy leaped from Edwina to Luna, grabbing for the hat before it flew off as the sleigh jolted into motion.

"I wonder how Rudy hooked up with the lions," she remarked.

"My fault. I needed help finding you, so I kind of promised him a lifetime supply of nuts."

"That will cost you. For a three-pound squirrel, that bugger eats a lot. The summer he fetched my daddy after I broke my leg jumping in the creek with Cousin Billy, we ran out of my mama's jam before winter finished. Thought my daddy was gonna cry."

"Sounds like he's been around a while."

"Yeah, which should be impossible given squirrels don't have the longest life span."

"I think Rudy might be special."

She leaned against him. "So are you. How did you know I needed rescue?"

"I didn't realize you were in trouble until I got to the farm."

Which led to the obvious question. "Why did you come to the farm?" After all, she was supposed to be on a plane to Florida.

"I had to see you. The moment I heard your flight got grounded, I realized I couldn't just let things end between us."

"There is no us."

"Not yet, but I'd like there to be."

"To what end? You're a prince. I'm a farmer."

"And? I didn't take you for a snob," he teased, only to yelp and hold on as the sled hit a bump and soared.

Oddly enough, there was nowhere else Edwina would rather be than snuggled with Felix in a seven-lion, one-wolf sleigh.

Until the singing started.

Luna belted out an ear-bursting Christmas melody —a la lion.

"Barreling through the snow,
   "A squirrel guiding the sleigh,
   "Lions and a wolf do pull,

"Roaring all the way."

To which Felix snorted. "More like puking because it's a bumpy ride."

Luna heard and stopped singing long enough to twist her head exorcist-style, roll her eyes, and say, "Don't be a pussy."

Apparently, Felix wasn't the only one with a problem. The lone wolf of the group uttered a sharp bark.

"Don't you start on me. I offered to let you drive, but no, apparently, I'm suddenly fucking fragile because I am carrying your child. Ha!" Luna burst into even fiercer song.

"Icicles on golden manes ting,
"Making fucking spirits bright.
"What fun it is to race and swerve
"To save a bear tonight."

At that, Edwina made a noise. "Okay, now that's going too far. I would have woken up in spring."

"Think you can do better? Go right ahead," Luna offered.

"If you insist. Let me see if I can remember the words my grandpa taught me." Edwina cleared her throat.

> *"Jingle bells, lions smell,*
> > *"But at least they're pulling a sleigh.*
> > *"About time those lazy cats*
> > *"Did more than sleep all day."*

"I hope you realize who you're antagonizing," Felix muttered as Luna huffed.

"Yeah, someone who's going to lose me a hundred bucks if she doesn't drop the kid before midnight," Edwina goaded, eyeing the belly that would pop anytime now. The winner stood to walk away with a nice five Gs. Edwina didn't actually need the cash; she just wanted to antagonize the lions.

"Is that all you got?" Luna taunted.

"The second verse has a part about shaving."

Felix winced. "Ouch."

"Sorry, I don't know any extolling the virtues of hair products."

"Enough flirting. More songs!" Luna's threat to serenade never came to pass, as the lions pulling the sleigh began roaring, and it oddly came out sounding like "Silent Night."

Edwina leaned against Felix, enjoying the surreal moment. Especially when they reached her house and Felix scooped her, blanket and all.

"I can walk," she protested—not very hard. She'd

not been swept up and carried since a young age. He did it with ease.

"You are not walking barefoot in the snow."

"I could shift."

"You could also be quiet because we're almost there." He headed for the door while the lions shook off the snow behind them.

"It's probably locked."

"That's not a lock," he retorted as he lifted his foot and kicked it open. It led to wild cheers behind them as his actions were noticed by the now shifted Pride.

"You can put me down now," she said as they entered a house that held a chill. She'd not been here to feed the stove and her backup heater required electricity, which had gone out again. She really needed to look into getting some solar installed.

"You need some warm clothes." He headed for the loft stairs.

"I should get the stove going first," she protested.

"Someone will light the fire."

Why did she keep arguing? If he wanted to carry her around, let him, especially since he didn't grumble and moan about his back.

She could hear the lions entering her home, their voices boisterous and lively, also worrisome.

"I'll get the fire going."

"You're not supposed to play with matches."

"My probation for that is over."

"Hand over that jug of vegetable oil."

Felix finally set her down, slowly, and she met his gaze.

"Thanks for bringing me home." A soft murmur.

"Is that my cue to leave?" Felix arched a brow.

"Do you want to leave?"

He snorted. "Do you really have to ask?" His hand cupped the back of her head. "There is nowhere I'd rather be."

A yodel from downstairs shattered the moment as Joan said, "I know where she hides the spiked cider."

Followed by Luna yelling, "No fair, you know I'm not allowed the hard stuff."

"Not our fault you won't pop that baby," her very brave husband said.

"I might have if you'd given it to me harder."

"I gave it to you four times!" he bellowed back. "I'm not a machine."

Edwina's lips quirked. "I don't think they're leaving."

"Some of them will. As many as can fit in Leo's truck. He's not missing Christmas with his kids. The rest will have to stay until they get some fuel for the snowmobiles."

He'd said "they," not "we."

"What about you?" she asked.

"Afraid you're stuck with me, Honeybear."

"I like sticky things," she said before kissing lips sweeter than honey.

Even better than honey, the sex that followed.

After sex, snuggles, on the last few hours before Christmas when, all through the house, all the lions were sleeping, even the terrified mouse.

Edwina, wearing nothing but a passed-out cat, had just settled down for a really good nap.

That got interrupted by a loud, "Who's that sleeping in my favorite chair?"

Papa Bear was home.

CHAPTER SEVENTEEN

HARK THE ANGRY FATHER YELLS...

Felix woke to Edwina shoving at him. "Wake up. Quick, get dressed."

"What's wrong?" he asked.

A woman's voice from downstairs exclaimed, "Who's been baking in my kitchen?"

"Someone drank from my mug." Papa Bear.

"A cat ran around with my yarn." Mama Bear.

It wasn't just Edwina's eyes that widened at the thud of feet hitting the stairs to the loft. Felix barely had time to yank on his briefs before a big man in a red and black plaid jacket with a bushy gray-streaked beard and matching brows confronted him in Edwina's bedroom.

The man who could only be Papa Bear pointed as he said, much too softly, "Gold-i-lion, you dare to sleep in my baby girl's bed?"

Like an idiot, he replied, "Only because it's just right."

Wrong answer. Papa's belly shook with fatherly rage before he dove for Felix.

An agile cat, he only still barely managed to dodge the massive paws that swiped while Edwina yelled, "Stop that right now, Daddy."

Felix didn't blame the father for going after him. If the roles were reversed, he'd have done the same. However, he would like to survive the night in a way that didn't require harming Edwina's father.

When the choice came to hit or flee, Felix flipped over the loft railing to the floor below, legs bent as he landed on his feet. He stood his ground, though, as Father Bear came pounding down the steps.

"Mangy tomcat sniffing around my precious baby girl." Papa Bear slammed a fist into an open palm as he advanced.

Edwina hollered, "Daddy, don't you dare crush him."

Given the glower on the man's face, Felix didn't hold much hope for his ribs if he got in his grip. "Sir, I swear I have nothing but respect for your daughter."

It did nothing to ease Papa Bear. "Should have known a sly lion was the reason why my baby didn't make her flight."

"I didn't make it because it was cancelled." Edwina came down the steps tying off her robe.

"And you didn't think to call?"

"I was busy, what with being tasered and left to die in the woods."

"What?!" Apparently, Dad thought Felix was to blame given the way the man charged. It almost resulted in a mauling, but thankfully, Mama Bear stepped in front of the angry father and, with no fear of the raging beast at her back, smiled at Felix.

"I'm Magda. And you are?"

It was the watching Luna, emerging from the kitchen with a cookie, who said, "Meet His Royal Majesty, Prince Felix Charlemagne the Seventh."

"A prince." Magda tittered. "Delighted to meet you."

"Like honey we are!" grumbled Papa Bear.

Mama Bear didn't even turn around. "Calm down, Eugene. Have a cookie."

"After I get rid of the scum defiling my baby girl." Papa cracked his knuckles.

"Dad, you know I'm thirty-five and not a virgin, right?" Edwina remarked tartly.

"Argh. My ears," the man blustered, slapping hands over them.

Edwina shook her head. "Says the man I caught chasing Mom around the orchard, threatening to spank his naughty shepherdess."

Ruddy color filled Eugene's cheeks. "That's different. We're married."

"And why don't you tell everyone how that happened?" Mama Bear stated with an arched brow.

"Don't forget the part where my father brought out his shotgun."

"Still got the gun." An older gent, who could only be Grandpa, held a long-barreled weapon and aimed it at Felix. "So, you gonna do the right thing, or am I burying you in the east orchard? No wait, that one's full. The west one."

"Grandpa! This is not the Dark Ages. You can't force him to marry me," Edwina huffed.

"Oh, honey," Grandpa cajoled. "Yes, I can."

"Is it because you think I'm so unlovable that no man would ever want to marry me himself?"

Grandpa gaped at her. "I never said—"

"I heard it!" Joan popped up from the couch and waved her hand. "He totally implied it. But I'm kind of torn. On the one hand, my feminist side says resist the patriarchy, but at the same time, I've never been to a shotgun wedding."

"I want to know where the popcorn is, because this is the most interesting Christmas morning I've ever seen," Luna commented from the kitchen.

"Ignore my husband and father, Your Majesty." Magda put her hand on his arm. "Would you like a coffee? Maybe some breakfast?"

"Indeed, I would. Call me Felix." He flashed a smile, managing to ignore the fact he only wore his briefs.

Magda tittered. "I can see why Edwina likes you."

"I never said I like him!" Edwina squeaked.

"You didn't have to." Magda winked.

"Hold on. We are not letting him off that easy." Grandpa's gun didn't lower. "I still want to know your intentions toward my granddaughter."

Before he could say she was his mate, Edwina slapped the gun down. "Put that thing away before you shoot your eye out," she chided.

Grandpa groaned. "And to think you're supposed to be my favorite granddaughter."

"I'm your only granddaughter, who is suddenly wondering how you got here if flights were canceled."

"We have our ways," was mother's inadequate reply.

"What ways? A magical blackhole? Because there's no way you could have driven in time either."

Jeoff chose that moment to lean in the doorframe of one of the bedrooms, disheveled as he finally roused from sleep. "What's going on? Is it the baby?"

"No." Luna glared at the hump.

It was Papa Bear who frowned and said, "What exactly is going on here? Why are there cats sleeping over? And what's this about Edwina being dumped in the woods?"

"Wolf over here." Jeoff waved. "And we're here because my mate and friends were helping the prince rescue Edwina. Alas, we got stuck because, as usual, they rushed off without thinking or enough fuel." Jeoff threw them under the snowmobile.

"I thought Edwina would have some in the barn," Luna retorted.

"Which turned out to be an erroneous assumption."

"Well, excuse me," Luna drawled. "Couldn't exactly ask her now, could I? She was unconscious in the woods."

"Would someone explain what happened?" Papa Bear roared.

Edwina patted his arm. "It's okay, Papa. I'm fine. Felix found me, and then the lions pulled me home in the sleigh. It was actually quite nice."

"Speaking of nice. When are we going after those naughty guys who stole the hives?" Luna dropped that tidbit, and Papa Bear's jaw just about hit the floor. Mama Bear braced herself on the kitchen island.

It was Grandpa who whispered, "Someone absconded with my honeybees?"

Edwina rushed to comfort the old man. "Don't worry. Soon as we get things sorted, I'm going to find them."

"We all will!" Luna announced, even as Jeoff bellowed, "You will not. I am putting my foot down."

Blame the shouting that followed, which explained how they missed the approaching rumble of an engine. When the headlights swept the living room window, all talk stopped.

"Who is that?" Papa asked.

Good question. Now what?

They stepped outside to see the snow had finally stopped and a large moving van was parked in the driveway. The passenger door opened, and a body trussed in designer scarves got tossed out to hit the ground with an, "Oof." The prone figure was then used as a stepping stool as a designer boot alighted.

It belonged to someone Felix knew.

"Mom?"

Indeed, his mother had arrived, and she didn't come alone. Francesca hopped out of the driver's side. "I told you he was fine. He's too annoying to actually die," his sister grumbled.

"You found Barry and the hives!" Edwina rushed past him to check the back of the truck.

Felix greeted his mother saying, "What are you doing here?"

"Can't a mother surprise her son on Christmas?"

"Of course, you can, but how did you know I was here?"

"I heard all about your adventure when I arrived to surprise you at Arik's condo. Which took forever given our plane was grounded at the wrong airport. We had to rent a car. Rent!" his mother railed. "Despite our paltry vehicular accommodation, the moment we heard of your plight from Arik, we set forth."

"But the roads, they're a mess," Felix sputtered.

His mother waved her hand. "We were fine until this truck almost took us out. Swerving all over the road when he pulled out abruptly from a truck stop.

We ended up stuck in a snowbank, and when I went to ask if the truck driver could render us some aid"—more like demand as she railed at him about his driving skills—"I found this human"—she nudged Barry with her foot—"ranting about the squirrel trying to kill him."

"Would this be a squirrel with a Santa hat by any chance?" Felix asked, despite knowing it was impossible for it to be Rudy.

"As a matter of fact, yes. Anyhow, when your sister smelled the honey in the back, she figured he was up to no good."

"I don't understand. Barry heisted the stuff hours ago. He should have been miles from here. And what of his accomplices?"

It was Francesca who had a reply. "There was just the one guy. And if I had to guess, he dumped his friends at the truck stop and spent the night, hoping the roads would improve."

"What should we do with him?" Felix asked.

"Excuse me." Papa Bear shoved his way through the lions to grab Barry and sling him over his shoulder. He trudged off in the direction of the barn.

Did Felix dare ask what was planned for the human?

Probably better he didn't know.

Since they were all awake, they chose to put the hives back into the barn, sealing it shut before Joan offered to take the truck somewhere to dump it.

As they watched the red taillights winking out of sight, Luna broke into song.

"Deck the mane with bells and ribbon."

THE LIONS FILLED in the chorus.

"Fa rawr rawr rawr rawr rawr rawr rawr rawr."
"Tis the season for some follies."
"Fa rawr rawr rawr rawr rawr rawr rawr rawr."
"Don we now our fur and claws."
"Fa rawr rawr rawr rawr rawr rawr rawr rawr."
"To decimate those who'd break our laws."
"Fa rawr rawr rawr rawr rawr rawr rawr rawr."

BEFORE THEY COULD START a third off-key verse, Luna suddenly clutched her belly and gasped. "Holy shit, my mother should have called me Mary, because my water just broke."

EPILOGUE

WHAT CUB IS THIS WHO CAME TO PLOP IN JEOFF'S HAND WHILE HIS MOTHER YELLED.

Luna's water broke in a tidal wave that soaked her feet and left everyone in shock.

"Holy crap on a cracker!" Jeoff yelled. "We need to get you to a doctor."

"No time," Luna grunted. "Baby is coming."

"What do you mean no time?" The poor man's voice hit a high note.

"Someone boil some water. Edwina, clean towels." Mama Bear didn't panic and knew just what to do.

At the stroke of midnight—with much cursing, swearing, and threats of severing Jeoff's manhood—baby Simba was born with what Felix declared to be the most perfect head of hair.

At the time.

. . .

A YEAR LATER...

The most perfect daughter in the world, Princess Lulu Honey Barkley-Charlemagne would celebrate her first Christmas—with the biggest tree Felix could find.

In Spain. Not his idea. After much fighting and crying, between him and his mother, Edwina put a stop to it saying, "I think Christmas in Spain instead of Florida sounds great. Your mother promised to put my family in a whole different wing from us."

When he'd initially dragged home the tree for his wife, Edwina had eyed it with skepticism given the sparse branches bent under the weight of the ornaments. But she still smiled and declared, "It's lovely."

"No, it's not. However, I have another present for you." He'd spent quite a bit of time on it. A whole year in fact. A year of wonder and happiness the likes he'd never imagined, because of Edwina.

"I don't need anything else. I've got everything I need right here." She snuggled in his arms.

"It's a gift from the heart. So try not to laugh too hard." He cleared his throat and began.

> "Felix, a prince from Europe, had some
>   really shiny hair,
> "And when he goes to America, he
>   almost loses it on a dare.
> "All of the other lions, like to laugh and
>   call him names,

> "They're all just really jealous of his
>   incredible mane.
> "Then one stormy Christmas week, a
>   blizzard came to play,
> "Felix got smushed by a falling tree
> "But a she-bear saved the day.
> "When a honey thief comes a stealing,
> "This princely lion saves the day,
> "And the lovely she-bear Edwina,
> "Finally lets him have his way."

"Not bad but it needs one more verse." She smirked.

"Please, as if you can make that more perfectly awful," he teased, wearing the ridiculously comfortable plaid pajamas she'd gotten him as a gift. Too hot this time of year in Spain unless he cranked the air conditioning in their bedroom, which suited his wife just fine. His in-laws, however, declared Spain a fantastic choice for the holidays, all of them, not just Christmas —to his mother's horror.

Just one big dysfunctional family. And he'd never been happier. Blame the woman who cleared her throat and straddled him as she sang.

> "The she-bear decides she loves him,
> "And marries him despite his quirks.
> "A good thing he's a skilled lover,
> "With a really humongous—"

He slapped a hand over her mouth and eyed the sleeping baby in her bassinet. "Is that really appropriate?"

"I was going to say mane." She smiled wickedly at him.

"Sure, you were."

She opened her eyes wide in not-so convincing innocence. "Are you saying you didn't like it?"

"It's perfect. Just like you."

His Christmas miracle, and only for her and his little princess would he deck his mane with ribbons and bells.

As the happy family celebrated Christmas, the squirrel who'd smuggled along in their luggage tilted his Santa cap and rubbed his little paws. Now where could he find some acorns?

AND THUS ENDS OUR LITTLE PRIDE-MAS STORY. I HOPE IT MADE YOU SMILE. MERRY CHRISTMAS. MAY YOUR HOLIDAYS BE RAWR-Y AND BRIGHT.

More books in A Lion's Pride:

Need some new shifters to love?

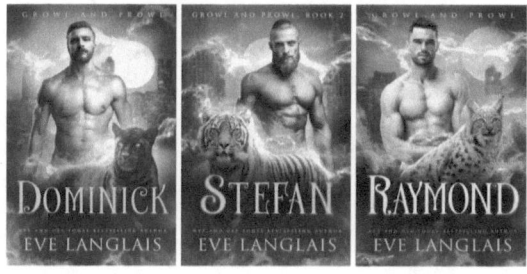

Be sure to visit www.EveLanglais for more books with furry heroes, or sign up for the Eve Langlais newsletter for notification about new stories or specials.

www.ingramcontent.com/pod-product-compliance
Lightning Source LLC
LaVergne TN
LVHW041634060526
838200LV00040B/1568